BOOK THREE OF THE CELTIC PROPHECY

Oracle's Curse

BY
MELISSA MACFIE

Can't Put It Down Books

Oracle's Curse
Book Three of The Celtic Prophecy
Copyright 2017 by Melissa Macfie

ISBN: 978-0-9994623-1-7
Printed in the United States of America

Published by
Can't Put It Down Books
An imprint of
Open Door Publications
2113 Stackhouse Dr.
Yardley, PA 19067
www.CantPutItDownBooks.com

Cover Design by Genevieve Lavo Cosdon,
www.lavodesign.com

This book is dedicated to my children, Elizabeth and Donald.
Remember that it takes sheer force of will to affect change in life.
Take a chance, experience new things, and breathe.

I love you.

"I am the master of my fate. I am the captain of my soul."

—*W.E. Henley*

Prologue

Death had come for her in its beauteous magnificence. Time slowed. Not in the usual self-contemplating way, though that was true enough; it slowed from Finvarra's working. The Oracle raised her eyes and saw a bird suspended motionless in the sky. *So this is how it ends*. She recognized it now. Arrogance and self-aggrandizement built slowly over the centuries bolstered by outside worship of her abilities had made her forget the fact that all things must come to an end, even her. Her death was the first of her premonitions, before even the official bestowal of the sight by Aerten, the goddess of prophecy.

She looked down at her open hands. Her gnarled, swollen joints made it impossible to extend her fingers. They were old hands, spotted and trembling; still useful in a perfunctory way, the yellowed nails embedded with dirt. How long had they been like that? She seemed to remember a point in her life when appearance meant something. Images of dainty hands, with clear, rounded, and most importantly, clean nails, that used to be hers flashed through her mind. She reached up to her damaged eye, wiping at the constant tearing. She didn't need to see it; she knew what it looked like. A milky, yellowish-white cornea almost indistinguishable against the sclera, if anyone bothered to look, was the brand of the seer, a lesser gift from Balor, the god of the Fomorians. It was praised as the seers' protection. No one would dare do harm to a seer whose powers lay in divination. Truth was no one dared to touch a seer at all. It was a lonely life. She had had to squash all hope for a family and children early on. She was venerated and ostracized.

Yet as the Oracle spent the last few moments contemplating her life's choices, a small part of her rebelled at the thought of fate and its importance. Hadn't she spent a large portion of the latter part of her life struggling against it? If anyone was going to have a shot at circumventing fate, shouldn't it have been her? She was there when Aileen had given her unborn child to the universe, an unprecedented move; it shouldn't even have been possible. The Rite of the Phoenix always had two willing participants for the sole purpose of perpetuating the faith.

Now, at this moment she hesitated. She wanted to simultaneously grovel at the feet of her gods begging for their beneficence and forgiveness so she'd be allowed to bask in their terrible beauty while at the same time standing defiantly as her lungs were robbed of their very breath, and she, all at once, was tried, convicted, and executed for heresy.

She looked at the priestess, the woman called Brenawyn, kneeling beside Aerten, touching her. The sight hardened the Oracle's resolve. Here was the so-named priestess, who hadn't been raised in the Ways, knew nothing of the lineage of the Druids. She was ignorant of the customs, rites, and hierarchy, and here she was touching the goddess of prophecy! The audacity!

With a harrumph, she stood taller and made her decision. The Oracle's interlace grew brighter as she chanted.

I curse ye, priestess
In the name o' Belanus, god o' healing
May he turn his face from you.

I curse ye, priestess
In the name o' Epona, goddess o' fertility
May she not hear yer silent empty-armed suffering.

I curse ye, priestess
In the name o' Danu, goddess o' the land
May ye never find a home.

I curse ye priestess
In the name o' Taranis, god o' the dead.
May ye live forever.

I curse ye, priestess
In the name o' Cernunnos, god o' the hunt
May ye never find what ye seek.

I curse ye, priestess
In the name of Blodevweld …

Chapter 1

Present Day

The pain abated as long as Maggie Harris remained utterly still and didn't breathe. That was a problem. Even in shallow breaths the pain radiating from her lower leg was excruciating. The way she laid on the floor she couldn't reach to explore the unseen damage, and to move to sit up—she'd rather not vomit again. She fluttered her eyes trying to clear her vision of the maroon blobs as soft flakes drifted to land on her cheeks. Dry blood. Assessing for lesser injuries, she found she had bled from a head wound at some point. There was an underlying throb, the real soreness of which was probably masked by the acute pain in her leg. She reached up to gingerly explore and found more dry blood covering half her face. It pooled around her head drenching the hair underneath. It was brittle, flaking away easily. How long had she been here?

Panic set in even though she knew that head wounds bleed profusely. She had never seen, or rather felt so much of her own blood. She jerked, and a bolt of lightning shot up from her leg. She screamed, reaching down to cradle her knee. The change of position opened the wound on her head and she felt a trickle of new blood ooze at her hairline. At this angle she could see the damage to her right leg. A memory of the life-sized skeletal model from anatomy class came rushing into her mind. Her tibia looked…odd. The weight of her jeans was almost too much to bear; to press on the fabric to get a better look at the shape of her leg required more courage than she had at the moment. She registered that the leg was broken.

Scuffling sounded from the room beyond, drawing Maggie up short. "Whose there?"

A slip of a girl appeared at the doorway, almost drowning in the huge pile of folded cloths that were clutched to her chest.

"I see that you're awake. That's good. I was beginning to worry."

At the muffled words, Maggie brightened, "Please, you have to help me. I've been kidnapped and taken I don't know where."

The moving pile of fabric stopped and teetered as the girl looked back. "He wouldn't like it."

"He's here? Near here? Where is here? Where am I?" The questions tumbled out of her mouth, each one pitched in a higher voice than the last. She stopped, realizing she was spooking the girl, who wavered, then ran to the corner, out of reach, and put the folded fabric on a wood chest in the corner. "Someone will be coming soon. I told him you needed a doctor. He didn't like that, but I think he's sent for one anyway."

"How long ago was that? Where am I? What does he…"

The questions tumbled out of Maggie's mouth again; she couldn't stop them once panic set in. Once again, the girl looked afraid, Maggie realized, noting her own panic reflected in the girl's eyes just before she skittered out of the room. There was real fear there.

Maggie's position was dire. She needed to think. He needed her alive for now, he'd not have taken her if that wasn't the case. What did she know? What did she have that he wanted?

Maggie's thoughts were cut off as soon as they began by the rushed thump-thump of multiple feet on stairs beyond her vision. In her pain-addled mind, a memory flashed of when she was eight. *The reverberation of the circus elephants' weight hit the arena's floor after being forced to do tricks for the audience. She was awestruck and scared at the enormity and power of the animals, and disgusted by the whips and bull-hooks the trainer's held. She felt the revulsion emanating for her mother's newest boyfriend as she tried to hide her eyes…*

Two men entered the room, followed by the slip of a girl again. They rushed her, and Maggie tried to cower away as much as her leg would allow. They had the advantage of being of sound body, and persisted, subduing her with little effort; a man pinning her shoulders as the girl pressed her hips down. The other man took his time searching in a black bag. He must be the doctor that had been sent for, Maggie thought.

He pulled out a syringe and a rubber-capped injection vial. "Relax. The pain will be better momentarily." He inserted the needle, pulled back on the plunger, and then tapped the barrel to rid it of any air bubbles. He gave a slight smile as he approached, possibly as an attempt to look less threatening, but Maggie wasn't having it. He had to know the circumstances, or at least could guess them given she was lying on the ground in a dirt floor basement. He couldn't be trusted. He wouldn't help her. She struggled even knowing her abysmal odds. She wasn't mobile, and even under the optimal conditions of a sterile hospital emergency room or an orthopedist's office to get a cast, she would only be partially so. Yes, she knew her odds and didn't like them a bit. At the moment she was completely at the mercy of her captors.

The smile on the man's lips disappeared as he knelt down on her side extending her right arm in a punishing grip. "You will cause yourself more pain if you continue to struggle."

"You see where I am. The circumstances, even if they aren't clear to you, you know, *you know*, I am not here willingly. How can you be an accomplice to kidnapping? You're a doctor! Doesn't that go against your oath, or something?"

He sat back on his haunches, "The Hippocratic Oath? No, there's no correlation. Plus, you aren't going to be harmed in my care. You're not going to die. This," indicating the syringe, "is only a local anesthetic so I can realign your bones. Unless," he shrugged his shoulders, "you want to suffer without. It will be much more painful. I wouldn't suggest it myself, since we have meds in abundance now. I shouldn't have liked to be a doctor in the past, setting bones, amputation…"

"Amputation? You're going to take my leg?"

"No, no, certainly not. It's a messy break—compound fracture from the looks of it, but I won't know until I take a better look. Will you allow me to take a look before I give you anesthesia to put your mind at ease? It will only take a moment."

Maggie found herself nodding agreement, and the pressure eased on her lower body as the doctor instructed the girl to retrieve his bag and extract the trauma shears. A few more instructions and a breathless, room-spinning moment the leg of her jeans was cut away.

"If you would, sir, please help her to sit up a bit."

Maggie was elevated, but the movement and the sight of the bone where it pierced her skin was enough to make her vomit on herself. The girl looked away, heaving in reaction, while the doctor looked on unconcerned, patiently waiting for her to stop. The only sympathy was from the man who helped her to sit. He moved behind her head, so when she finally eased back it was to rest on his upper legs. He brushed her bangs off her forehead, but stopped midway to yank back his hands as if caught doing something he shouldn't. Maggie looked at him for the first time. He was young, her age if she had to guess. Lanky, and wiry strong, and with a short scruff indicating a week's worth of beard growth. Underneath that however, was skin that hadn't exactly resolved itself of pubescent acne. She tried to memorize his face, holding him in her stare as long as possible, letting him see the tears that spilled from the corners of her eyes. She had to make an impression, for this boy might be her only help.

"Despite the look of it, the break is clean; and I'll leave you with a couple of blister packs of antibiotic. You aren't allergic to penicillin, are you?"

Maggie nodded, "I get hives."

"More and more people are developing allergies." He said more to himself than her. "Any more that I should know about?"

She shook her head. "Very well. I am prepared in any case. Keflex should knock out any infection that starts." He took the syringe back from the young man, and flicked it again for good measure. "Shall I give you the local now?"

Maggie came to sometime later in the basement, but things had changed. Gone was the dry blood, and there were fresh stitches at her hairline. There was a cast on her injured leg and she was divested of her jeans, all of her clothes in fact. Someone had taken the time to wash her, comb her hair, and dress her in a loose linen dress that skimmed her calves. She lay on an army cot that smelled of disinfectant and she was covered with a thin, hospital-issue knit blanket.

She startled when someone cleared their throat. She turned her head to find the young man balanced on a spindled chair against the wall. Her stomach growled at the sight of the folding snack tray laden with food and bottled water next to him.

"You're awake. Do you want some water? You must be thirsty."

She nodded and went to sit up. As her feet brushed the ground, a wave of dizziness hit her and the floor rushed up to meet her. She was saved by two strong hands steadying her back on the cot. "Are you okay?"

Maggie sighed deeply, unable to focus. "I'm…fuzzy-headed." She looked down to his hand still clutching her shoulder. She could feel the warmth of him through the fabric of her dress, could almost count the nerve-endings set off by the tingly, pins and needles under his touch. His hands were large, with big knuckles; she reached and poked his index finger. "Do you crack your knuckles? My mother always warned me not to because I'd get large knuckles."

"You're not making any sense, lie back down."

"What did he give me? I feel…floaty."

"Enjoy it, because the meds are wearing off and the pain will come back soon enough. He'll want to see you then."

"He? Oh yeah…him. Cormac Mc-something or other."

"Yes, and he's not happy."

"Probably still angry at me for hitting him in the nuts with a bat."

The young man snorted in agreement.

"It was a really good swing. Haven't played since high school. Do you think I would have had more power if it was aluminum rather than wood?"

He leaned in, "Jesus, girl, shut your mouth, he's looking for payback. If you want to make it out alive…"

She grasped at him, "Please help me. He took me. He's keeping me here against my will. Won't you help me get away?"

"Hush now, close your eyes." He laid her head on the pillow and swept up her legs up, "Just sleep," he said, covering her with the blanket.

"What's your name?"

"I'm Andrew. Andy. Call me Andy."

All Maggie could do was nod and lie there, mollified by the comforting weight of the blanket. She concentrated on her breathing, fascinated by the rise of her chest as air filled her lungs. She held her breath and then exhaled slowly, delighting in the ease of pressure. It seemed a difficult task, the inhaling, such labor to force air in, to expand—what if she forgot to breathe? In her relaxation, her body just gave up?

What had the doctor given her? It was time to get off the loopy train. She had enough…but it was just so nice to just…be.

She should concentrate on something else. Rafters. Planking of the floors above, what was significant about this? Something was missing. She wished she knew what. Insulation. Shouldn't there be insulation? Was there typically insulation on the ceiling of basements? Or would it invite mold? She suddenly wished to be more observant. She certainly would have seen it in the basement of Leo's shop. That was a couple hundred years old at least, but it was updated, now that she thought about it. Mr. Callahan updated it for his wife, all except the still room. That had been left purposely untouched. She always thought it was funny why Leo had wanted it that way, but she never asked why. There's that unobservant bit again, or maybe she considered it unimportant or just crazy eccentricities of an old woman. She never asked, though with the happenings of the last couple of weeks, she should have asked if its untouched state had anything to do with the existence of magic. Maggie wondered if she'd ever get a chance to ask now.

Going down that road seemed dangerous considering her addled state, best to think of something else—ooh, pretty spider! The bright yellow and black spider stuck out against the dark backdrop of the aged rafters, busily finishing its enormous web anchored at several spots along the jagged walls of the corner, it stretched across two ceiling beams. The spider looked huge, as if Maggie reached out she could pluck it off its web. The color and pattern were extraordinary, and almost made her forget her revulsion for the arachnids in her desire to look closer at it.

A stray memory of her ex-boyfriend laughing as she stood in the hallway throwing shoes into her kitchen hoping to squash the spider on the floor. It seemed ridiculous now; how accurate did she think she was going to be throwing random shoes, rubber boots. She thought she even remembered a soft-soled slipper, from ten feet away? She wouldn't even step into the kitchen. It was Tommy who had saved the day, or he would have if he hadn't dropped it down her shirt afterwards. He swore that it was dead, but who does that regardless? He was always a little shit. She felt itchy. She located her yellow nemesis in the same spot it had been; her skin crawled just from the memory. And to think, she wanted to touch this one. Euck!

Maggie woke again, this time to a deep ache in her leg and a throbbing from her forehead. The pain helped to sober her and allowed her to think straight. Her wounds had been seen to at least. Whatever Cormac had in mind surely he needed her at least for the time being, else why would he have her injuries seen to?

People were in a cast from four to six weeks. The more time he needed her alive, the more time she had to think of a way to escape. She certainly couldn't expect to get away quickly in her current state.

The chair back creaked at her back, "Maggie? Are you awake?"

Her heart leapt in her chest and she felt the anxiety rise; no, she needed more time to think. Andy seemed like he was a compassionate sort, and it was a good bet to take that he'd let her sleep some more. Although he was mixed up with Cormac, so he clearly couldn't be trusted. She wished she had a better bead on what was happening. She lengthened her breathing, feigning sleep and banking on the fact that it would stave off the inevitable confrontation with Cormac himself.

Thinking back to when the blinders were peeled from her eyes just weeks ago with glowing orbs, resurrections, shape-shifting, not to mention time slowing, dirt monsters, force fields, and fucking gods! Her heart was beating fast and panic was surging. It was harder to concentrate to keep her breathing relaxed. It hardly seemed possible that she was still sane and alive, but magic was real.

Magic was real.

Nothing was going to be the same again.

She could use a little of that magic now to get out of her current predicament. Before Cormac showed up would be preferable, but it was unlikely to happen. She saw Leo and Brenawyn raise Alex from the dead, but here her captors had to call for a doctor to fix her broken leg. Healing must not be a common ability, or whatever they needed her for wasn't pressing, or they didn't want to expend the energy to heal her through magic—too many questions. Quite honestly, it was a path she didn't want to go down, she had no family outside of Brenawyn and Leo, and she wasn't sure where either of them were, if they were even still alive. If they were able they would call the police to report her abduction; but what would they tell them? Leaving out details would certainly make them look suspicious, but they couldn't tell them what actually happened. That would result in a 72-hour stint in the psych ward.

What did the police tell families of abductees? The first twenty-four hours was crucial? She didn't know how much time had passed but she was at least a couple of days in and that speculation was built on the time she was conscious enough to notice the light in the grimy cellar window.

She had angered him in the forest. She took a chance and it hadn't worked out. He was clearly rattled by the turn of events in the clearing and the decision to take her was a rash one. She thought she could use that. Make herself hard to kidnap, and perhaps he'd think better of it. She tried to gouge his eyes, and stomp his instep, she managed to get away for a moment. It was a mad dash through the underbrush, but he was better equipped, with rugged boots and jeans, and he overtook her almost instantly. Crashing with her to the rough ground, crushing her, before both of them took a tumble down a short decline. She was winded but in one piece, but he was quicker. A sharp pain at her temple and she drifted off thinking this is where she was going to die.

Now that she was conscious, and the meds were wearing off she needed to compose herself. The time was coming when she would need her wits about her. It wouldn't be good to further anger Cormac. He had no compunction about causing pain. The next time might be more grievous. She didn't know how she came to be here, but she could be observant from here on out. There might be something that she'd recognize, not so much in landmarks, but towns and people. People were nosy; less apt to get involved in a situation they knew nothing about, but there might be an opportunity.

That brought her thoughts back to what she already knew about her situation. Maggie had seen the doctor, the girl, and Andy. The doctor wasn't going to help. He'd made that clear enough, and the girl was too scared. That left Andy. She knew she could exploit his nature, manipulating him into helping her but she had to be sure that she was right about him. She had to establish a rapport with him. He had been sitting vigil in the room while she slept and had food and water, offered the latter to her already. That's where she would start; ask for basic needs to be met. She was thirsty.

Chapter 2

Tir-Na-Nog

Alex wasn't physically chained as he was led from the forest clearing by Cernunnos, God of the Wilderness, Lord Master of the Wild Hunt, but he was compelled to go nonetheless. He was bound to it as the hunted. He had never much minded until now, when it felt as if each step toward his destiny was a step away from the last chance of his happiness. He watched Brenawyn for as long as he could, walking backward through the veil surrounded by slaughs, the hounds of the Hunt. He had no faith, nor trust in the gods; he had been warned specifically by one of them, but he was forced to leave Brenawyn in their care. He was afraid that this would be the last time he'd see her, that she wouldn't make it off the field, but have her heart's blood drain into the earth, and never feel the weight of their child grow heavy within her. She should know happiness at least.

He wanted to rail against the forces that be, scream to the cosmos how unfair it all was, but they were uncaring as time itself. He had to muster hope though, at least until Samhain, the date she was to surrender herself to Cernunnos. Alex would rather die a thousand more deaths or become a gancanagh than subject her to whatever torments awaited her with the god. Cernunnos was the father of her soul, but the deity had no capacity for love beyond the hedonistic desires of the mortal realm. What he wanted with her, Alex couldn't imagine.

The atmosphere changed as darkness fell over Tir-Na-Nog. The temperature dropped and the trees grew closer, with moss-laden entwined branches and thick bracken underneath. The slaughs drew closer together, but there was a tension in the group, a sense of heightened anticipation. They bumped his legs, and he could feel that tension in their muscles, a strained hesitation to leap at him, tearing with their teeth; they were waiting for the call to begin.

Their gait quickened, nipping and growling at each other; they were excited. Alex knew that sound. They sounded much like dogs before the bugle signaling the fox hunt. He had heard it too often, the sound of the slaughs gearing up for a chase. Only the slaughs wouldn't retire at night in front of a fire or in a heated, cushioned bed nestled at their master's feet. No, the slaughs were immense by comparison, large like a black bear, with two rows of canine teeth so large they couldn't close their mouths, leaving them always slavering, yearning for something they would never get, no matter how many hunts they ran. They had been human once, foolish enough to strike a bargain with one god or another, but when payment came due, they couldn't pay. This was their punishment.

Even though Alex knew from whence they originated, he couldn't spare an ounce of pity for them. Being ripped apart by those teeth and claws were reminders enough that they were so far gone it mattered naught that they were once men. They were demons now, and demons they would remain for the rest of eternity.

The long straight back of Cernunnos sitting on his steed, outdistanced them for most of the journey, but at last he stopped and turned to wait for Alex. When Alex gained on him, the slaughs were jumping and baying, eager for the commencement, but with a hand signal, the demons calmed.

"Reliquary, ye ken I made a promise ta the priestess, no' ta let danger come ta ye 'afore Samhain. I plan ta keep my word, but I need yers in return. For ye see, the Hunt has been awakened, and t'will be difficult ta stay their hand e'en temporarily."

"Aye, what dae I need ta dae?"

He dismounted and approached. "Any show o' dominance will be kent as aggression." The slaughs melted from his path as he circled Alex. Cernunnos tapped his shoulders, "Slouch," and kicked the back of his knee, "and kneel, eyes cast down a' all times. Mumble minimally in response only when spoken ta. Make yerself as small as possible, the object is no' ta look like a worthy adversary. These—they ken ye. They'll be eager."

"Aye. That I ken well."

"This defiance o' the Hunt has ne'er been attempted 'afore. I must ponder the ramifications."

"T'is no' like I'll be killed in the process. Let me run the course. T'will be done and o'er 'afore the priestess is due, with her none the wiser."

"A promise made is a promise kept. Ye will keep in the meantime. Another will be called up in yer stead. Jan Tregeagle, methinks, would make a good substitute. He is hated in equal measures with how yer prized."

"Doonae flatter me, t'is just the same in the end, death then resurrection."

"Reliquary, ye are unique ta this forum, distinctive due ta yer office—ye are the sole mortal that can lay claim ta being gifted from the gods each time."

"Aye, I am just better prey."

"Tregeagle cannae claim as much."

Alex knew what Cernunnos was saying, but he still thought Tregeagle had the better deal. In his limited, albeit, wily ways, the magistrate should know that there was no hope of victory against the gods. He may have been a king among mortals, but he was a maggot in the midst of the gods, to be squashed without a thought.

It was true what Cernunnos said though, Tregeagle was hated, and the only other who was called up as much to run the Hunt. On occasion, Alex was paired with him for the gods' amusement. He knew firsthand the conniving man couldn't be trusted, he'd have sold his own mother to earn an advantage, but it was his ambition that incensed the gods, ambition that drove him to aspire to more than his mortal station.

Each took their pleasure in crushing the life from Tregeagle's lungs and in the moment of death, resignation was the only thing reflected in his eyes. But in Alex's case, every time he came back, it was to be stronger, faster, infused with magical abilities, and with it hope that one day he'd best the Hunters, even Cernunnos himself. That was Alex's true punishment, because that hope was unfounded. To delay the inevitable was torture because the Hunt for him was his drug. He craved its high, the resurrection, the awakening to when all things were new again in the instant before ability was born.

Cernunnos motioned, "Och, here they come. Be ready."

Alex assumed the position of captive as the group approached like mist settling over the hills. From his lowered graze he recognized Gwyn ap Nudd, with his red-eared white hounds, Wild Edric, the rebel Saxon, and the antlered helm announced Herne the Hunter. Arthur Pendragon was present as well as others who had earned their place in the company at great personal cost.

There was movement from the back and the company parted to reveal Ruadan, the Formorian spy. He was an arrogant bastard, a cruel and determined Hunter, one who wouldn't accept defeat. A warrior from birth, a true Colossus in his time, now made impotent by the Covenant. He was relegated to the Hunt, a compromise that probably would have seemed fitting to those who drew up the contract to his history and honors. They might have seen it as befitting a warrior, but it was a death sentence to one so gifted. The Hunting Grounds were his golden cage.

Ruadan stopped in front of Alex, addressing Cernunnos. "Good, brother, ye ha' brought a worthy opponent. T'is been some time. Shall we commence?"

"Nay brother, no' this time. He is bound in the terms o' parley that ha' been granted."

"Unacceptable. Those bound ta the Grounds cannae be bargained with. Ye ken this. The rules cannae be broken or amended. They were made 'afore us and will remain e'er afterward."

"I decree it."

"Ye cannae defy fate, e'en if I were ta agree."

"All the same. Ye will yield, and call another ta sate the desires o' the Hunt."

Ruadan's nostrils flared and he moved so his feet were planted shoulder width apart, hands hung at his sides loosely but his knuckles flexed. He was a head shorter than Cernunnos, but wider in the shoulders and more stockily built with a blacksmith's forearms and biceps knotted with muscle. "Perchance t'is time for a change in leadership?"

"Och, and yer the one ta dae it?" Cernunnos looked around at those assembled. "Does anyone else agree?"

Looking hesitant, they nervously looked away, Alex noticed. These were the wildly rash, deadliest predators who managed to make the cut to be in the most elite group of hunters, but they still thought it best to keep out of the power struggle unfolding before them.

Ruadan made up his mind as he exhaled, and ran at Cernunnos who braced for impact with his antlered head lowered. Ruadan was quick and swerved to avoid being skewered. He came away with a scratch to his cheek, but managed to get his hands around Cernunnos' neck, relying solely on the strength of his hands to choke him into submission, for death was impossible even when god was pitted against god. All either could hope for was a tap out after exhaustion took hold at the end of a very long struggle.

It was clear from that moment though, that Cernunnos wasn't interested in a drawn-out battle of wills; he employed a compression blow to Ruadan' ears, unbalancing him, and followed with a head butt to break his nose. Ruadan' hold broke as he cradled his injured face, allowing Cernunnos to spin him around and slip his arms underneath his armpits and lock his hands behind his head. Cernunnos applied pressure, pushing his head toward his chest and using the advantage of the height difference to lift Ruadan off the ground. With the restriction of air flow from the broken nose and the additional pressure from the submission hold, the fight left Ruadan quickly and he slumped in Cernunnos' arms.

Cernunnos held on though, probably from experience with his opponent, Alex thought. This was for all ostensible purposes, a mutiny, and Cernunnos had to show strength or else have his authority tested at every turn here after. How many times had this happened, he wondered, if not from Ruadan, but others in the group? He looked about, all assembled were formidable, some former mortals like Pendragon who had gained admittance through improbable feats; others were lesser gods, not physically capable of overpowering Cernunnos. There might have been murmurs of discontent, but not many contenders beyond Ruadan in the group. A thought occurred to Alex at that moment. Was the entire group in attendance?

Cernunnos threw Ruadan' body to the ground and sneered at his prone form before striding toward his horse to get the curved ram horn strung over the pommel of the saddle. He looked at Alex with a slight smile and then at Ruadan, "Come, ride with us. For tonight, ye are a Hunter."

Chapter 3

I curse ye, priestess
In the name o' Cernunnos, god o' the hunt
May ye never find what ye seek.

September 1457

William Sinclair, the laird of the Keep, bowed and led Brenawyn to a seat on his right. "So my lady, what is it that ye seek? And how may we help ye in yer quest?"

Before she could formulate an answer there was movement, and the crowd amiably parted. A tall, fair-haired man walked forward, his head down. The over-sized linen shirt and baggy pants couldn't hide his lean muscular physique. Recognition dawned as Brenawyn registered him as the father of the little girl who had come to her room; she clung now to his knees. She smiled. The girl must be happy her father was home. The smile faded because something was off. The way he stood, his stance was peculiar: feet planted a shoulder-width apart, back poker straight, hands balled into fists. It reminded her of someone … he lifted his face to her.

The metallic taste of blood, a loose molar, I breathed in through my mouth—broken molar, an exposed nerve, but no pain there. The pain radiated lower, my back screamed, pressure on my stomach. That was me. I inhaled sharply to move, praying that I could still do it, dreading the wave of new explosions of agony once I did. A scream that hardly sounded like it came from within me escaped my lips. Sweating. Shaking. Assessing. Broken tooth and wrist. Hurt to breathe. Broken ribs? The baby! My hands went to my belly, hard as usual. Interminable seconds and ... nothing. I pushed on my stomach expecting, praying for an answering pressure. None. I felt lower, my hand came back covered in blood.

The stairs creaked with his slow step. His face came into her field of vision. His strong brow and cheekbones, his dimpled chin, blue eyes she'd thought to be the color of the clear ocean, now the color of ice, devoid of all emotion.

Her mouth went dry, new beads of sweat formed on her brow, her heart felt like it would burst from her chest. "Liam!" Brenawyn hissed wrenching herself out from beneath Sinclair's grasp and pivoted away. "You're dead. I buried you, you son of a bitch!"

Liam vaulted onto the dais but was blocked by a befuddled Sinclair. "Let me past! Ye may think ye found the priestess ... they may think they've found the sleeping lady; but in truth t'is only my wife ye've found."

Brenawyn clasped her hands to stem the trembling, but her anxiety spilled over in the tears she shed. She wanted to run, scream, hit someone as she stared at the face of her abuser, her husband—the man she had buried years ago. In her head she knew what he had done, but she had the remnants of the memory binding too, making her doubt herself. When she found out originally it had been so easy to give over to it, mourn the loss of her child, hate herself for so easily forgetting even though it wasn't in her control; but now looking at Liam she searched the face she had memorized for some hint there were tender feelings for her, but all that stared back was cold and hard. Anger and contempt welled in her gut.

William grabbed Liam by the collar as he lunged for Brenawyn. "Yer wife?"

The incredulity dripping from Sinclair's accented voice drew Brenawyn up short as she remembered where—when she was.

"Aye, it seems as if t'were in another time, another place; but that is my Brenawyn."

A scream filled the hall. It took a while for Brenawyn to figure out it wasn't from her, but the girl.

"Guards! Clear the floor. Hall is over. Escort everyone out o' hall."

This might be her only chance to beg for help because women didn't have the same rights here. She sputtered, grabbing, clinging to Sinclair's sleeve, "He beat me, led me to believe he was dead, tried to kill me…"

"Yer his wife, no' many will interfere. Most will think t'is his job ta discipline ye." But Sinclair swung on Liam. "Is this true?"

No response.

"Answer me."

"Aye, she believed me dead for three years."

"Why man?

"I wanted rid o' her."

"Then by all means, she is nay longer yer concern." Pushing him off the dais, and turning toward Brenawyn, "Milady," he said, "ye passed the requisite time o' separation. Ye are no longer married ta this man if ye wish it so."

Brenawyn nodded because she couldn't trust herself to speak. She wanted to throw herself in William's arms, her savior at this moment, and cower behind him.

"Escort the Lady ta my solar; and ha' McAllister tossed out." He shouted, but he jumped down off the dais and stalked over to where Liam was. "Doonae go far, man. I will be coming for ye shortly." He turned and in the same tone, instructed another guard to post watch over him until he came. "Dae something with his girl, too. At least take her out and calm her."

Brenawyn was being ushered out by the same guard who brought her down to hall. *His girl? He was a father? How could that be? She was what, ten years old? How the hell did time travel work? Did he have her beforehand? Afterward? She didn't understand, and there was no one who could explain it to her, because she as sure as Hell wasn't going to give anyone else any information. She'd end up dead, and she might even deserve it too, if she managed to make it through the day.*

Alex, where are you?

Brenawyn needed to regroup. Reassess what she knew about where she was. What, if anything, she could disclose; she'd need to come up with a story before long.

She arrived at the door to the solar in moments, piloted in by a gentle yet strong hand at the small of her back, and closed within, without a word said. The door locked behind her. She should have been outraged by being locked in, but she was glad to have the protection of the oak door between her and whatever dangers lay beyond.

It was quiet in the room, well-kept, and manly. These were Sinclair's personal chambers. There was no reason to put her here other than it offered proximal security. She didn't think that many saw the inside of this room, so the wealth of the trappings could not be for spectacle. The coffered ceilings and bookcases were of the same dark wood which was so well-oiled it shone in the setting sun's light granted by the diamond-paned windows. Brenawyn went over to one and looked out. Not having the availability of mass manufacture, these had to be crafted individually and represented hours of exhaustive work to produce something so exquisite in its imperfection.

She was too far up to consider crawling out the window, even had it been wide enough. Escape this way was impossible. She ran her fingers over the nearest book to her right, pulling it out of place, leafing through it and marveling at its hand-illuminated pages. The next book offered the same, and the third a product of a printing press. Brenawyn had a flash of one of her students, Christina, nervously standing in front of the class presenting her interdisciplinary project. *Was that really just a few months ago?* The girl had drawn Johannes Gutenberg and the printing press. At the time, Brenawyn thought she would lose her mind listening to monotonous recitations; but something had stuck. She was glad of it because at least it gave her a reference point. *How many times did she tell her students that they never knew when information would come in handy?* Whenever she was, it had to be after 1440.

The bookcases ran the entire length of the room, stuffed with similar volumes. A map of the region hung over the massive, cold fireplace at the far end. The stone mantle was flanked by two overstuffed wingback chairs with a table in between.

Movement had Brenawyn turn to the chair facing the fireplace, and a large grey snout came into view.

"Well, hello there, puppy."

A *thwap, thwap,* of its tail on the seat, was her answer. She circled the chair to see a large shaggy grey hound curled impossibly tight on the chair. Only then did he unfold himself and come to sniff her hand. "Oh, you're a handsome boy!" She scratched him behind the ear, and he half closed his eyes as he leaned into her. "Like that do you? So does my Spencer. I wish he were here now, but you'll do."

She didn't have much time. She needed to find out as much information from her surroundings while she was alone because paying inordinate attention to her environment might draw more attention to that fact that she didn't fit in. She was in enough danger as it was. It was fortuitous that she was locked into his study. The oak desk beckoned to be ransacked. Not a hospitable move, but necessary. She didn't want to move anything, in case he noticed. His desk was efficient. A short stack of prized paper lay off to the side with an ink well, quill, and a stub of wax, with what she thought to be his seal situated in easy access. There was a ledger that lay on the other side with sealed envelopes on top. She took a swift look at the door, and down at the dog who stood by her side, panting. "It's just a quick look. You won't tell, will you?"

Brenawyn took the letters off and flipped open the book to the last entry…September 1457. Her hands trembled. 1457.

What in the world made her agree to this? Her mind flashed back to Alex floating face down in the pond, and the ridiculous promise she made to an impossible figure, a faerie, for Christ's sake, to save his life. It had seemed like a dream. She recognized that she made her promise based on heightened emotions, but this was no promise to God that she'd go to church more often. She had made those before. Promised God she'd be a good girl if he brought her mom back, saved her dad from his heart attack, or much later be more devout if he'd allow Liam to live. Hers was not a god that took direct action, though she tried her best to be a good Catholic. Her current situation was more than she bargained for. She had accepted the mantle of some official office she knew nothing of, and the next thing she knew she was whisked off to serve in that capacity. In 1457!

Hysterics bubbled up from her gut, and she was cackling and crying at once. A soft scuff on the other side of the door had her clamp a hand to her mouth. She put the letters back on the journal, adjusting the stack to resemble what she remembered, and quickly dashed to the chair facing the fire. The dog followed in tow, and the minute she was situated he draped himself over her lap.

There was something reassuring about his warm weight that rooted her spiraling thoughts to the spot. *Pet the dog. Pet the dog. It's not that bad.* The dog would be wary if there was anything amiss. Animals were like that, even if he wasn't hers. As long as he was relaxed and lounging on her there was no immediate danger. They stayed in that position for a long time, and Brenawyn's heart eased feeling the steady beat of the dog's and the cadence of his breathing.

The grate of the key in the lock pierced the stillness and woke the dog, which readjusted on her. Even her gathered skirts, petticoats, and whatever else she had on as undergarments didn't protect her fully from his massive paws as they dug in between the muscles of her thighs so he could peer over the back of the chair to look at the intruder. He whined a bit, and the tail thumped in response.

"Dunmor, come."

The dog clumsily jumped down, and Brenawyn felt defenseless and bare, the sudden chill in his absence echoing the tightening knot in her stomach.

"Would ye like some claret, lass?"

Not wanting to appear demanding, she answered, "Only if you're pouring yourself some."

"Och, nay for me. I doonae touch the wine. Makes my head ache. I'm a Scotch man, myself."

"Well, if you're pouring, I'd rather that instead."

William chuckled. "Ah, I should ha' guessed myself that Alex would ally himself with a woman o' good taste."

The dog circled back and sat at Brenawyn's feet as she turned to face William who eased into the chair opposite her. He scowled as he handed her the glass.

"You can tell that just from my drink preference?"

"Well, nay, no' exactly, but I doonae ha' much ta go on now, dae I. My dog likes ye, at least. Sometimes I trust him o'er my advisors, such discerning taste he has."

"And this distresses you?" She quickly shut her mouth and shifted her eyes away from him, intent on finding the bottom of her glass in a vain attempt to control her responses. Women were not so bold now.

"*Hmpf*," he grumbled. "Let me summarize for ye then. I am called away from an extended hunt ta come back ta my Keep because the Sleeping Lady appeared o' a sudden. I get here and am made ta hear o' the circumstances o' her appearance and how she was pitiful confused and in strange garb. She mistakes me for my brother, but that is only after I decide ta offer my protection and a cover story for prying eyes. Ta make things worse, as I arrange ta dae things proper-like and introduce her in Hall, she demonstrates magic for all ta see, healing a child—thank ye for that, if her mam didnae think ta offer it; but are ye daft?" He waved a hand in dismissal, "Ne'ermind that now. And then one o' my tacksmen claims that she is his wife, though I cannae see how that came ta be since t'is clear ta all that ye are no' from anywhere near here. Did I miss anything, my lady?"

"Just that I thought Liam was dead. I buried him—thought I buried him...I did bury someone."

"Aye, I remember, ye *said* that."

"You don't believe me?"

"No' o' itself, nay, I wouldnae, though ye did look quite shocked ta see him, that's true enough."

"Then why?"

"I ha' some reason ta believe McAllister. He's been known ta me since we were young. Though, ye could ha' knocked me over with a feather ta learn that he has two wives!"

Brenawyn was startled at this revelation. "What?"

"Ye'd ha' no' reason ta ha' met her. I was told ye hadn't been out o' the Keep since ye've arrived. Is that nay so?"

"I haven't been outside. Just the turret room and what you call Hall, and I've always been escorted to and from."

"Aye. For yer protection, and ours, truth be kent."

"For your protection? How do you see that I'm a threat?"

"I dae no' see it, but I ha' the care o' all who live here."

"I understand, I do, but it still leaves me—

"Aye, it dae." William nodded his head in agreement. "So ye're wondering what I am going ta dae with ye? For the moment, I've sent McAllister on an errand that t'will keep him a fortnight. In that time,

I expect the local magistrate and the bishop ta arrive."

"Oh?"

"There is some danger for ye, and that cannae be helped. Ye were verra public in yer demonstrations, so while I've had ta formally request that the bishop come ta keep the peace, I ha' staggered the missives. The magistrate will arrive sooner, and he will determine which o' the marriages is valid."

"It's the marriage with the other woman—what is her name?"

"Then ye kent about it 'afore?" William looked at her questioningly.

"No. I am just not going to contest it. You heard him. He wanted rid of me. He faked his death to be done with me. Plus, he has a d…daughter."

"That makes it easier. Ye'll be able ta leave all the quicker."

"Leave? Not that I'm not grateful, that I'll be allowed to leave, but I've no idea where to go from here."

"As much as that intrigues me, if ye're here when the bishop gets here, by then he'll ha' heard o' yer exploits with the child. He'll bring witch hunters."

"Oh shit, then that's my cue to go."

"Ye'll go with the magistrate, Amergin. He'll know what ta dae. He is a friend o' Alex. He'll keep ye safe, safer than I can keep ye here, e'en with my title as clan leader."

Chapter 4

Maggie made a show of struggling to sit up, but in truth, it was awkward with her leg immobilized. She had to relieve herself; there was no point in tip-toeing around it. It was either ask for help or soil the cot.

"Help." she called pitifully.

Andy peeked around the door frame, "Yes?"

"I need to...um… I need to use the toilet." She feigned modesty. "Can you get the other girl to help me?"

"She's busy at the moment. I'll help you. I am…was…was an orderly at New York Pres…"

She must have given something away because he clamped his lips shut immediately. She could kick herself. She'd make a terrible interrogator. She could always control her mouth, but she could never control her facial expressions. So he had ties in New York. Perhaps that meant they were still in the state.

He frowned and disappeared, calling out, "I'll be right there."

Maggie heard heavy objects being dragged and thought that he was clearing a path to the staircase and she'd be carted upstairs. This was a break, for reconnaissance purposes; perhaps she'd be able to discern her location. She didn't think it would happen so soon; but she was disappointed when Andy brought in a bedside commode for her use.

"Hold on, let me get set up. I'll get you situated, and leave you alone to make your toilette."

The word seems utterly ridiculous coming out of his mouth in an exaggerated accent, but she saw it as an attempt to lighten the situation. She made an amused snort.

He hoisted her up, and helped her across the room to the portable toilet and went to lift the hem of her dress. She went rigid, acutely aware of her vulnerability. Someone had undressed her after the local took effect, and left her without undergarments.

She could feel the heat radiating from his cheeks, as he clumsily made his apologies, and dropped the fabric. "I think you can take it from here." He retreated, tossing her a roll of toilet paper, before he disappeared around the door frame once again.

She had to be careful, but opportunity never just happened for her. If she wanted out, then she had to orchestrate it, and in order to do that she had to play the part. When making the decision to appear beholden to her captor, Andy, she thought it would be harder, but he found her attractive. He had restraint, or at least he had so far. How far did she take it though, before imploring him to turn a blind eye? To help her escape?

Wait.

What the hell was she thinking? She couldn't trust him. Whatever he told her, whatever he had done previously, he was mental. He was a kidnapper. She was out of her league, best to just try not to be killed.

Her new vantage point in the basement gave her more of an idea of the size of the place she was in. The foundation looked newer on this side, a clear color and size distinction in the type of brick used here. That could explain the chopped-up layout too. There was a doorway, but it was more of a hole chopped out of the original foundation; with no header to stabilize it, bits were crumbling away. Someone had swept the broken mortar into piles along either side of the threshold to keep the entrance clear. Maybe that was because of her presence here.

There was a well in the midst of the new space less than an arm's length from where she perched. Thank God, the near absence of light had made it indistinguishable from her previous location on the cot, else nightmares of creatures from beneath would have invaded her drugged sleep. Now, she thought sardonically, they will. Of course, that was in addition to the actual danger that lay with her captors. She craned her neck to look over the rim to see if there were actually creatures waiting beneath to slither up over the rim and across the floor, or scurry across the ceiling's beams.

Yep, that's better—attribute additional insectoid traits to what lurks in the dark! She launched herself up from the toilet seat eager to get away from the pit, and gyrated 180 degrees in an ungainly fashion until she caught her balance. The sharp pain at the break radiated out, and made spots dance in her vision. She reached out to catch herself before she fell, but the only thing within reach was the commode. It went down with her, splashing the contents of the bowl on the skirt of her dress.

At the clamor, Andy came rushing in. "Damn it. Why didn't you call me?" he said, hoisting her up from her armpits. He was scrawny, but she could feel the lithe muscles as he lifted her up from the floor. She was thin, but she couldn't offer any help due to the cast, and he hefted her without grunting.

"Let me get you to the cot. What were you thinking?"

Irate, and in pain, Maggie sniped, "I was thinking that I could finish taking a piss in private."

"You could have injured yourself further. At least you landed on your good leg."

Andy eased her down to sit on the cot. His hand went to her hip and Maggie froze. "Relax. I'm not going to hurt you."

Maggie scoffed.

With a hand on her shoulder, he lifted her legs and pivoted her to position them on the cot. "I'm trying to see if you did, in fact, hurt yourself. Lie back."

Beads of sweat formed on her brow, knowing that if he wanted to hurt her there was little she could do to stop him.

He probed her hip joint and knee in a professional manner, but when he took hold to bend the leg, the skirt rose up. Maggie quickly balled the fabric in her fists, shoving it down to cover her nakedness.

He reached down to the foot of the cot to drag up the blanket and gave it to her. "Arrange it however you want to preserve your modesty," he said a little sarcastically as he sat back on his heels. "It's in your best interest for me to check it out, though. The doctor's been paid a shitload of money to hang around, but the agreement ends tonight."

"What happens after tonight?"

"We won't be seeing him again, for one thing."

"What's going to happen to me?"

"Nothing for the time being, until you're healed."

"And then?"

Andy sighed and rose to his feet. Looking down at Maggie, "Me and Carolyn are to keep you here, fed and hydrated."

Maggie knew she was pushing it, trying to extract information from him. She could tell that he was shutting down, but she couldn't stop herself. "Until when?"

He strolled away to the far side of the room and righted the upturned commode. Now that Maggie knew what was there, she could easily make out the shapes. He leaned back against the well wall, crossing his ankles. "That's for Cormac to say. He has not let on what his timetable is."

He must have shifted his weight and the stress was too much on the old bricks. It started with bits of loose mortar pinging off the bricks, and then the upper bricks caved in under him. Maggie reacted, but she was too slow only managing to move to a sitting position.

The tumbling bricks echoed as they hit the interior wall, until finally splashing at the bottom. He barely caught himself before he tumbled after and looked back to see that the first three rows of brick on that side crumbled away into the bottom of the well. They both exhaled simultaneously; Andy ran his hands through his hair probably thankful not to have gone over, and Maggie holding her chest relieved that her one hope of getting out, albeit a remote one, was still alive.

Andy backed away, "Holy shit that was close! Fucking creepy-ass well," more to himself than Maggie. He was visibly shaking when he approached to sit next to her.

"Are you okay?" Maggie felt she had to act concerned if the ruse of getting him to eventually help her was to succeed.

"Yes, of course. I should have known better. This whole place is falling down."

"What the hell is it doing inside?"

"My guess? That it was originally an outside well, but with the various additions to the house, it was enclosed. Probably was a relief to the owners to not have to go outside to retrieve water, but maybe the house had running water already. Eh, who knows! Do I look like a historian to you?"

Maggie just shrugged, and her stomach growled.

"Where has my brain been? You're hungry. How could you not be? You've been here three days."

That sobered her. Three days. Three. And she was still alive. Had her wounds taken care of. Fed, or would be momentarily. But three days—hope took a hit. The more time that passed the less likely rescue would be made from outside. She needed Andy. She needed to make him help her.

A bottle of green tea and a plastic-sealed, convenience store sandwich were handed to her. "If you're still hungry there's more where that came from."

Maggie nodded, ripping open the wrapper with her teeth. The sandwich was delicious, though she had previously avoided those sandwiches before, not finding their presentation appealing. A second was placed on the bed next to her, and she opened that one before she had swallowed the last bite of the first. She guzzled the tea, and only half registered the fact that she was making gluttonous noises. She didn't care. Finally, she sat back and burped, wiping at her mouth with the back of her hand.

"Are you done? Do you want another sandwich? A drink?"

"I'm good, thank you."

Andy took the wrappers, stuffed them in the empty bottle, and threw it in the well. He turned to her and shrugged, "Nothing but net."

Maggie had thought he was older than she, she couldn't tell from the full beard and poor light, but perhaps he wasn't as old as she thought he was.

He went to the doorway, and stuck his neck through, keeping a hand on the wall. "Cormac, when you're done. She's ready for you."

Chapter 5

The crowd parted and a horse was brought forward for Alex. Beads of sweat broke out on his brow because this beast was one of Cernunnos' own herd: twenty-two hands, sleek, midnight black, red eyes, and razor hooves. He could feel those hooves as if the wounds had been just inflicted, trampling him, crushing bone and organ before the last blow that crushed his skull. When was that? A dozen resurrections ago? They made a lasting impression even though the wounds had healed, and the scars long since vanished. It had no ill-will towards him, but Alex remembered. He squashed down any hesitation and swung up into the saddle. Divine or not, the horse had to know who the master was, else he'd be thrown and actually might end up trampled again.

Alex looked around at those assembled, reflecting on the choices that brought him to this very moment in time. He couldn't help but feel that he would just complicate his life and make a veritable enemy in Ruadan by accepting Cernunnos' invitation. How does one refuse a god, particularly the god to whom he is a bound slave? Alex had no choice but to acquiesce and deal with the fall out later.

Cernunnos blew the horn, and Alex's deific

bloodlust responded, his sigils igniting. He felt the primal instincts of bear, wolf, leopard and hawk together, but he remained in human form. He fought the urge to run with the slaughs and hounds, to be part of the pack when they got the scent of their prey. The necessity of the chase, the exhilaration of running the prey to ground, the taste of the spurting blood sweetened with adrenaline; all was an aphrodisiac of immense proportions.

While he still had the ability to reason, he chose to fight the pull of the animal, because once he gave over it would be hunt, gorge, mate, and sleep, in that order; and without Brenawyn...the thought of sex was unappealing.

Two riders flanked him. "Welcome ta ye, Sinclair, first time on this side o' the Hunt." Edric clapped him on the shoulder. Pendragon, a man of few words, nodded.

"Aye, thank ye, gentlemen, but I ha' ye ken now that I remember e'ery instance where t'were yer blade that cut me down."

The two exchanged an anxious look, "Dae we ha' ta settle this now 'afore the chase, or would yer honor be abated if we were ta wait until after?"

Amused and taken aback by their nervousness, Alex soothed, "Let us speak plain. I hold no ill will ta either o' ye. In fact, t'is for what ye did that I should thank ye. It made me what I am."

"T'is good then." Pendragon said. "Edric here

likes the aftermath best methinks, for he indulges like the newly initiated e'en though he has been here longer than I. Stays the longest in the arms o' the welcoming fold."

"Always a rebel, I am. Cannae resist the reckless abandon o' those that would welcome home a conquering hero."

"Stop blathering on about yer conquests, old man. They dae that for the whole contingent, or are ye daft? Come on, man, ye ha' ta know that their feeding off ye!"

"Visited by the dearg due, are ye then?" Alex ascertained.

Pendragon chuckled and punched Edric in the shoulder.

Edric huffed and mumbled, "Aye, but I am no' the only one that partakes o' their wares. They can glamour ta look like any bounteous beauty or," he lowered his voice and leaned toward Pendragon, "a familiar sweet face."

If he had wanted a rise out of the man, the effect wasn't apparent. He went on, "Besides, Arthur, here, his tastes differ greatly. Ye think that he'd like the battle o' it considering," he waved is arm in Pendragon's direction, "e'erything; but nay, he likes the moments after the kill, after the blood has stopped flowing—says he likes the quietude."

This did get a rise out of Pendragon. "Ta each his

own, Edric. I doonae feel I need ta explain myself ta ye, ol' fool if e'er there was one, but mayhap Sinclair will ken what I am speaking o'. Ye've beaten yer foe, or ye've spilt yer seed inta yer woman, there is a moment, small though it may be, that a sort o' exultant exhaustion washes o'er ye. In that instance there is nay thought o' the next conquest, the next item on yer agenda. Ye are at peace."

"Yer a woman, Pendragon. A weeping, helpless woman!" Edric interjected. "Unfit for the Hunt. Next time I hope its ye who angers the Horned One. Mayhap, being prey will give ye the stones that ye seem ta be missing."

"Come at me, Edric. I'd make swift work o' ye."

Sensing the shift in atmosphere, Alex looked around and observed the slaughs and hounds stop and bay in unison. "Hold!"

Edric took off, a battle cry screeching from his throat. But, Alex held out a hand to Pendragon. "I ken o' what ye speak. We are alike, more than ye ken." With that he kneed his horse into action, and took off in pursuit, bloodlust pumping in his veins.

He leaned low over the pommel, letting the horse have the rein, relishing the wild abandon and reckless speed. They ate up the ground. There was an evident dominant hierarchy in the run pattern that only a trained eye could see. As King of the Hunt, Cernunnos sat astride the alpha horse, by far the largest of the herd. From his vantage point, Alex could tell quite a bit about its body language and what it communicated to the rest of the pack. The ears were constantly changing position, one ear cocked to the back listening for what was happening behind it, both back now listening to direction from his rider, then pinned back lunging to bite one of the others who pushed too close.

Alex's horse was bringing up the rear so his ears faced forward intent on the hunt, until Alex put his hand on the steed's neck. He felt the shift in attention, the rise of hesitation, the ears twitched back and forth. The animal was confused; it was pulled in two different directions: the ingrained knowledge from the herd's hierarchical pecking order and the introduction of the apex predator instinct. The new direction was one of dominance, heightened smell and sight, the Way of the Predator. It battled and won over the horse's instinctual flight response, its primary defense, the first obstacle. It battered at the dominance conditioning, unraveling the herd mentality, the last of its resistance.

The horse snorted and blew its answer finally, and Alex felt it give over to him allowing him to transfer the predator traits to it. He felt the horse's stride lengthen with the smell of Ruadan burning in its olfactory glands. He felt its stomach growl at the traces of blood left from the struggle with Cernunnos. He felt its impatience as each hoof pounded into the earth.

Alex was weak; he knew he shouldn't give over to

shifting himself, he knew he shouldn't even have gone this far, to bask in the glory of the imminent kill. But while the memory of Brenawyn burned bright her importance to him faded in the moment. He was beast as the hunted, just as he was learning he was beast as the hunter.

The horse threw its head in the air to get a better line of sight, knowing that the slaughs and the hounds were leading the group slightly astray. It chomped at the bit to take lead and run the quarry to ground without delay. Alex let it advance and overtake the nearest riders. Most were those of long-forgotten renown. Pendragon would be among them in Alex's mind except for the stories told to him of the king's exploits when he was just a boy; Edric, would be forgotten too, too, but for Alex's propensity for liking rebellion stories.

He briefly registered their look of alarm when he blew past them, intent on getting to the front of the brigade. He passed remnant slaughs and hounds that broke from the pack and mulled around, noses to the ground, intent on picking up the smell again. He squeezed his legs against the sides of the horse and took a tighter grip on the reins, seating himself more firmly for the disturbance in the gait as the horse trampled a hound too slow to get out of their way. A solitary cry punctuated the drone of the Hunt: the clinking of armament and saddle gear, the blowing of horses, the yips and whines of the dogs, but he drove on.

He was drawing attention from the other hunters as he drew closer to the lead. They instinctually fell back wanting to stay clear of reprisals at so clear a breach of protocol. Alex urged the horse on, fueling its inner rage further, and the horse responded. Biting, kicking, and lunging, he made his way through the remainder of the herd to Cernunnos. The Horned One turned in time to see Alex advancing, and then craned his neck back to see the others give him wide berth. Cernunnos scowled at him. Alex had a vague recollection that it wasn't a good sign, but his reasoning ability was greatly diminished by his bloodlust. The Hunt was now in Alex's veins and would only be sated with spilt blood.

They came to a break in the hedge on Alex's left and the horse jumped the distance, breaking with the group. Ruadan was closer now, they both could smell him—the sweet nectar of the divine, a commonality amongst immortals, the smell of their sweat was part of their allure to mortals; and mixed with it was a minute measure of fear. Alex almost laughed aloud, Ruadan, the great Formorian, afraid? This emboldened Alex. Craning his neck to see the group in the distance, he couldn't believe his luck. On his first Hunt he'd be the one to bring the quarry down. He raised his own battle cry, an amalgamation of apex predators, and broke through the tree line on Ruadan' heels.

Chapter 6

As Sinclair escorted Brenawyn back to the tower room she couldn't help but notice the guards in tow.

"Am I to be kept under watch?"

"Aye, yer movements will unfortunately ha' ta be limited. First, ta keep ye out o' Liam's circle. His wife, his daughter, his friends; he's made a home here and I'll no' ha' ye upsetting the Keep by yer presence."

"But I've said I will not!"

He held up a hand to stop her. "Ye've said, but a woman's jealousy is another matter."

"If you were to say angry, resentful, humiliated, then maybe you'd have an argument." Brenawyn walked on considering, "And afraid. I'm afraid of him definitely—but jealous—not that. She can have him."

"And learning that he gave another woman a child, whilst yer own was…lost?"

She swiveled and glared at him, slamming her hands on his chest to bar him from going further, to stop picking at her insecurities. "How dare you!"

She should not have done it. She was sure that she could handle any ramifications for the slight, but she wasn't ready for his reaction. He covered her hands giving them a reassuring squeeze, and his eyes, so like his brother's, spoke the pity he felt for her.

"Even then, yer not jealous?" He lifted a hand and wiped away a tear that rolled down her face. "Nay, my lady, ye cannae control yer emotions with me, and I mean ye no ill will. I didnae mention it ta get a rise out o' ye."

Brenawyn scoffed.

"Or ta force ye ta dae something unwise."

"He has a lot of friends here?"

"He is well-liked, hard-working, and a braw fighter. I ha' nay complaints."

"Then why don't you dismiss me out of hand? Take his side?"

"I didnae get ta where I am by just taking how things look ta be on the surface. Each o' us has two sides, or more with some, but ta simplify matters let's just say it's two for the purposes o' this conversation. A public self that ye allow other people ta see, because like it or no' we need ta live in groups for shelter, safety, disbursement o' jobs, and the like. I'll get back ta this later, but life is hard. Many doonae make it long. Sickness, starvation, invasion, and even the weather seem like they're waiting just over the horizon with Finvarra o' old, the God of Death, ta claim the next soul. So we make compromises ta fit in. More times than nay, I believe because I am an optimist, ye see, that the public side reflects the private beliefs. This is just supposition though, because I cannae, nor ye, nor even the Oracles can with any surety, deign what is in someone's heart. I cannae tell what lies between a man and a woman."

"That's still true in my ti—I mean, where I'm from."

He raised an eyebrow, but must have decided to let it be, because he continued. "A man can lay hands on his wife, t'is the law. She is his responsibility ta discipline whether she is wont ta be a termagant or does something."

"Let me stop you there. Please do not justify a man hitting his wife."

"I think I'd like ta visit where yer from. Perhaps it's more civilized, or are ye an Amazon in disguise?"

"That's the first time I've been called an Amazon."

"Ah then, ye are familiar with the tomes."

"I am, though only in translation.'

"Ye can read, but ye doonae ha' the Greek. Yer education was lacking. What o' Latin? The Gaelic?"

"Not the first time I've been told that recently," she said, thinking back to her conversation with Nimue, the goddess of the moon in Tir-Na-Nog, who accused her of the same thing, only that time it was knowledge of the precepts of Druidism. "I have rudimentary understanding of Latin, but we're getting off the point. Where I'm from, I suppose you'd consider it more civilized. We have laws that prohibit domestic abuse."

William nodded in understanding and resumed his

stroll along the parapet. "Liam admitted ta wanting out o' the marriage contract, but how he chose ta handle it was the coward's way—so unlike the man I ken. It leads me ta believe that what ye've said might hold some truth."

Brenawyn was relieved to hear him say so. In a foreign place and time it was the first sign of good fortune. She could only imagine what her fate would have been if Sinclair deemed otherwise.

"Onto the second reason…"

Brenawyn almost forgot that there were multiple reasons Sinclair wanted to keep her under guard because she was still so shocked at Liam's apparent resurrection.

William stopped and looked out over the expanse, sighing, "This land has magic in her."

Brenawyn stood at his side, "It is beautiful."

"Thank ye, lass. Long, long ago before the coming o' the Romans it was a much different place. To read the stories, it was a land of wonder where the gods walked among men. I think it was a simpler time in one regard. Things were definite, if some god were to be angry, the people kent it immediately. Punishment was quick and fierce, but honest, and usually temporary. What most o' them wanted from us was ta be worshipped. Acknowledged and prayed ta in the correct way, each had his own preference," he laughed, "I suppose as dae all o' us. They were individuals prone ta peculiarities o' such."

"Go on."

"The Druids were peacemakers—orators, diplomats, law makers. There was no problem they couldnae solve with words. They had no definition of violence within their ranks. There were only three castes o' Druids originally. First was the vate, these were seers ta divine meaning o' the gods' will. The second was the priest, who conducted rituals and ceremonies honoring the gods. Third was the bard, whose job it was ta pass knowledge on ta the young so they in turn could carry forth the customs."

"I met a vate. I was *not* impressed."

"Did ye now? Ye'll ha' ta tell me about that some other time."

Brenawyn's thoughts were in a jumble. She'd have to concoct an amended story to tell him if he pressed the issue later, leaving out her direct involvement and that of her grandmother. Revealing that Leo was a Druid might not be seen in so great a light. It might just be another nail in the coffin, or tinder on the pyre that could be her death knell. She'd keep that to herself, but out of sheer curiosity she wondered which of the three Leo was.

"And Alex is a priest?"

William turned to her, looking through her to something only he could see.

"You did know he is…"

"Och, aye, for certainty. What he is, is largely by

his own making, the clod."

"How so?"

"He is the Reliquary."

"That explains nothing."

"He was o' the warrior caste, a later edition due ta the difficulties they had with the Romans."

"Things are starting to make more sense."

"By the time he was born though, the gods had long since retired to Tir-Na-Nog and the Romans soldiers were dust in their graves. The new caste stood as silent sentinels existing only because it honored those that fought and died a' the hands o' the invaders. He would have served never seeing battle o' those proportions free ta live his life here, but he had ta go and be typical Alexander."

"What happened?"

"It wasnae so long ago that things changed, and the night it happened was the start. We held the ritual here; the gods came, they still have claim ta a limited hold in this realm allowing some ta come and go. T'is a big energy expense, but they use it gladly for ceremonial purposes. Remember, they want ta be worshipped above all else. So, that night was the official installation o' Alex and some others ta full warrior. Alex was always the best hunter amongst the clan. His aim was true and he was quick about it. He also bested the other lads a' any contest and it made him cocky, thinking himself indispensable. Well, I wasnae there ta see it myself, but different accounts all relay the same. He was reveling in the honor of being newly appointed, he was emboldened thinking the gods thought him ta be indispensable as well. He reached out and touched the goddess o' prophecy."

"And?"

"And? He touched her without being given permission."

"I'm sorry, but I don't understand." Hadn't she done the same when she, if it was the same faery, had seized? She didn't know there was protocol.

"Because of his audacity, he was made Reliquary. The living collection o' all the lore o' the Druids, and his office is ta defend it with his life; so he is priest, ta be emissary ta the gods, performing the rituals in observation and be their physical form here in this realm. He is bard, ta teach those that come the stories; and he is warrior, man and beast able ta defend it."

"He is not his own man."

"Nay, through his own foolish means, and he's paid dearly already."

"So, how did that set things in motion?"

"The gods need ta be worshipped. It is the source o' their power, and when they had ta retreat ta Tir-Na-Nog mankind had ta fend for themselves. Man's innovation and ingenuity grew a' alarming rates because the gods were no longer present ta provide. Prayer stayed the longest out o' repetition, but the prayers answered became fewer, and the time between each became longer. The frequency o' prayer dropped, and there was no punishment forthcoming. People thought their gods had abandoned them, so they turned ta other answers."

"Let me guess, Christianity."

"Aye, and for a while, both existed, but with all things, this was short lived. Resentment for unanswered prayers tuned ta anger and hostility. What was once tolerable was now abhorrent."

"And this is your second reason for my imprisonment."

"T'is no' imprison—

"No. Relax, I get it. I foolishly showed my powers to a roomful of strangers, some of whom could be..." Brenawyn trailed off.

"Aye. They can be. I cannae say what is in their hearts. We have suffered in the past, and I cannae ken how it has affected them. They are my people, and we live in harmony more or less, but ye are an outsider, a stranger, and a priestess ta gods most doonae acknowledge anymore."

Chapter 7

The cellar door creaked open; of course, stereotypically, it had to creak. She was in an abandoned house, in all probability miles from any people; there was probably a lakeside camp nearby with stories of a roaming homicidal maniac, too. There *was* a cavernous well—Maggie was caught in a bad horror movie in the making. Noting the irony of her situation did nothing to abate her anxiety. Her mouth dried and her hands shook more at each of the interloper's heavy footsteps descending into her prison. She would come face to face with Cormac again, but this time there would be no way for her to resist him with the cast on her leg.

Andy looked worried, and he motioned for her to be calm. What the fuck did he know? He wasn't the one being kept against his will. She tried to focus on the irony again, it helped, kept her mind working, a sand shovel against the tide, but Maggie would take it even for a few precious seconds before the panic attack surged and all rational thought was impossible.

Eleven, twelve, thirteen, how long was that set of stairs? Fourteen. She was breathing faster and shallower. Her heart raced. Her muscles tensed. Her chest constricted. And then he was in the door frame.

"I should ha' just cut yer throat in the forest." Cormac declared as he looked her over. "Little use I fear ye'll be, and too heavy a burden."

Gulping for air, Maggie squeaked out, "Then let me go. Leave me here to get out on my own."

"Alas, I cannae. T'was ye or the old woman. Ye ha' no magic but still a strong connection ta…"

"To who? Brenawyn?"

"Aye."

Sweat was dripping from her brow, beads of perspiration slid down her cleavage making her yank at the loose dress. "You're mistaken. I mean nothing to her. I'm not family. I'm not even a friend. All I was…am…was a clerk in her grandmother's store. I don't even know if I still have a job. You've fucked up that place good."

"Prevarication is useless."

"Huh?"

Cormac raged toward her. "Doonae lie ta me! Did ye no' think we watched the house. We ken what ye mean ta her. She'll dae as we dictate if it means havin' ye safe."

Breathless, Maggie probed, "Do you even know where she is?"

He groaned in frustration, raking his fingers through his hair, "I ken where she'll be," he said, turning to Andy. "Get her ready ta move. T'is no' safe for any o' us ta be seen outside. I ha' secured other arrangements."

Andy nodded and followed him to the room beyond.

Spots were dancing in Maggie's vision, and if she didn't get her breathing under control she'd pass out from hyperventilating. She cupped her hands over her nose and mouth concentrating on employing deep breathing techniques to regulate her intake. The pounding of blood in her ears felt as if it would squeeze the last bit of air from her lungs and her heart would finally explode. She knew it wasn't rational, that she should be eavesdropping on the men's conversation in the next room, but she was going to die here on the cot.

Get breathing under control. In, out, in, out; don't gulp the air! Chest pains will ease when breathing is measured. In, out. In, out through the fingers.

The chest constriction eased, and her first instinct was to remove her hands to take a gulp of air. She fought the urge and remained as she was concentrating on oxygen regulation.

"…she ha' told me ye've spent all o' yer time down here. Is that true?"

"Yes. I thought you wanted me to…"

"She's bonny, is she no?"

"Well…I guess…"

"O' course she is. Young, clear skin, sun-kissed cheeks. Perky breasts, too small for my tastes but nicely-formed…and long legs. Did ye no' notice when ye helped strip her o' her clothing?"

Andy made an appreciative sound, and Cormac continued. "Ha' ye ever had a lass like her?"

Maggie didn't like where the conversation was going, but the direction shifted.

"Did she ask about yer life? Seem attentive? Ask ye why ye were involved in this? Beg ye ta help her?"

There was silence, then, "Oh, um…in that exact order almost."

"She's trying ta manipulate ye, lad."

"She is? I don't think she would do that."

Maggie could hardly hear his responses, his enunciation grew muddier, and the volume lowered. *Shit, that's not good. Rejection makes men do things.*

"She's yer test. The Oracle herself foresaw it, that ye would face many trials in yer initiation. This is yer first. She's a temptation."

Cormac's baritone rang out clear and true almost as if he wanted her to overhear him.

"What do I do? Maybe you should reassign me. Have Carolyn or Linda take my place."

"Is that what ye want, ta disappoint me?"

"No, no, of course not, but what if I'm…weak?"

"Och, lad, dae ye think I wasnae in yer position once? Ye ha' ta reflect on what yer heart is telling ye."

"I want to serve you, Master."

"Aye?"

"I want the Auld Ways restored."

"And?"

"I want to transcend."

"Then if that is the case, ye need ta be diligent because reward does no' come ta those who doonae work for it."

"I understand."

Maggie's hope died.

Chapter 8

Alex's heart beat in sync with the horse's, but he strained against its hesitation when he felt it slow. He urged it on but the horses' instincts took precedent for fear of miss stepping in the denser flora of the forest floor. In his right mind he'd know that horses were not predators, and while this one currently had the bloodlust, it was not in its nature to pursue.

Alex leapt off, tearing at his clothes, letting the shift override logic; the need to stay human forgotten. His bones lengthened and the wolf's stifle and hock were fully formed before hitting the ground running apace with the horse. Fur sprouted and covered his new body like dominoes falling. Last was the lengthening of the jaw, Alex gnashed his teeth as the canines grew. Of all the physical changes that he went through, the teeth always were the most lasting pain. They left his mouth bloody and raw from new teeth ripping through the gums, and the subsequent tearing through prey's flesh was electricity on a live nerve. It made him live in the moment, so vividly aware of his surroundings, the smell of the heart's blood pumping out, the final death knell that so closely imitates orgasm, death, and excrement that immediately follows.

He overtook the horse, plunging into the undergrowth; olfactory senses filled with the smell of Ruadan. He was close. He could feel in the pads of his paws each frenzied step reverberating off the spongy ground. He could smell the blood from the skirmish with Cernunnos, and the new scratches obtained from branches cutting at his skin.

On either side the undergrowth exploded with wolves joining the chase, falling in behind the alpha. They moved in unison, turning in murmurations much like those of starlings, connected collectively to Alex's mind. His senses grew wider. He knew where Ruadan was ahead, could anticipate his movement, but he also knew where everyone else from the hunting party was, too. Hounds, slaughs, horses, men, gods. He knew how much each carried on his person, the weight of the hunting tackle, the saddles—there were six coins in Edric's right pocket, *odd since the coins held no monetary value here*—and the weight of each member compressing the earth under them.

There was a growing echo in each footfall telling Alex that they were nearing the cliffs at the edge of the Hunting Grounds. Ruadan was slowing, too, his heartbeat was strong, but there was a slight tremor in his gait. His muscles were reaching their limits. He'd have figured it out by now, soon he would have to turn and fight it out. All this Alex gleaned from his paw pads.

The murmuration of wolves changed, spreading

out, the stragglers going wide and taking up outermost positions ahead of the alpha as they burst through the tree line. Ruadan was crouched ready with his back against the cliff's sheer face. "Come on, ye bastard! Come a' me!"

The wolves crouched low to the ground and held the semi-circle position guarding against escape as Alex advanced. Ruadan made the first lunging move, but Alex was quicker and bounded out of reach, more balanced on four legs. Alex sprang at him, finding purchase and sinking his teeth into the arm of the god. It wasn't a good hold, but first blood was drawn. Ruadan shook him off as if he were a lapdog instead of a twelve-stone wolf. Alex hit the ground on his side, the wind knocked out of him, but he regained his feet in an instant.

A thunder clap sounding from behind announced the arrival of Cernunnos and the rest of the hunting party. All froze except the wolves, which still hunched and growled at Ruadan.

Cernunnos dismounted and approached the nearest wolf and touched its shoulder. The animal squirmed away to keep line of sight with the prey causing the God of the Hunt, the God of the Wild to press his rights. "Disband."

The wolves' concentration was disrupted, one shaking its head, but they all held their formation.

"I say, disband!" Cernunnos bellowed.

This time there was movement, a skittering of confused animal whimpers, and tails tucked between legs, they scattered in all directions. Cernunnos did not move to face Ruadan or Alex until the last of the underbrush settled from the wolves' hasty departure.

"Concede, brother. The Hunt is lost for ye. Ye ha' been routed and all but captured."

"The rules were no' adhered ta."

"That is why I ha' ended it now. Acknowledge me as Hunt Master, and ye'll be shown proper respect for yer rank and position. Dae no' and in this moment I'll strip ye of yer immortality and ha' ye ripped apart for the duration o' this Hunt. Think on it. Resurrected o'er and o'er, repeating the chase until ye concede. What say ye?"

Ruadan looked at Alex, his wolf jowls still slavering, nothing holding him back but the will of the god, and thought better of it. Alex, he knew, was the willing servant of Cernunnos and he would at the god's behest run him to ground repeatedly, not to mention the personal satisfaction that he would get out of being able to set the beast free here, not concerned about the carnage caused, or blood split, because there was no authority except the rules of the Hunt; unrelenting, savage rules, but within them a wide berth of acceptable behavior. Until he was clear of offense and appeased Cernunnos' ire, Ruadan would be subject to the brutality of the hunter.

Ruadan bowed low, "Aye, Master o' the Hunt, I

concede."

Alex couldn't believe his ears. After all this he wasn't going to be allowed the kill! The bloodlust raged in his veins, and he raised his head and howled for his pack to return.

Cernunnos ignored Alex, and announced to the group, "Let us retire ta the Great Hall for revelries and feasting!" Then turning to Alex, "Come, I will deliver ye personally ta the bath house, as only those honored by the kill ha' e'er visited."

Mounting his horse, Cernunnos led the way through to a path not before traveled, and Alex still in wolf form followed because his horse wasn't provided. The journey was silent. Cernunnos kept quiet, and raging emotions boiled in Alex's mind. He still heard Ruadan' heartbeat, still smelled the sweet scent of the divine laced with tangy fear, and wanted, beyond anything in his recollection, to taste more of it. He salivated continuously, but he wasn't going to be allowed to make the kill.

The wolves reappeared and fell into formation behind Alex. Cernunnos didn't turn, but addressed the new additions. "Interesting that. T'would under different circumstances be investigated…and dealt with, aye."

Alex seethed.

"The priestess, my daughter is found. Ye ha' all but delivered her yerself. This is my reward ta ye, and yet ye treat me with... dare I say it? Defiance bordering on mutiny. Did ye just no' see what I dae in the face o' rebellion?

Alex wanted nothing more than to sink his teeth in and crush a windpipe, feeling the blood pumping out to quench his thirst.

"We will continue this discussion when ye've sated yer lust. Here we are. Come. I will introduce ye."

Cernunnos dismounted, throwing the reins over the horse's head, and led the way to a towering tree with a large hollow. At its widest point it could have allowed both of them to proceed shoulder to shoulder, but the Cernunnos had to twist to allow for his antlered helm to pass, and Alex still in wolf form, entered afterward.

The immediate interior was spacious; Alex's enhanced hearing picked up the hoot of an owl and its owlets in the expanse above. At the center of what should have been a dead tree, was the top of a spiral staircase leading down. Beyond the first few steps, the staircase widened allowing Cernunnos to pass unrestricted. The stairs wound through the roots of the tree above and the further they descended the more ornate the railings became. Carvings depicting pastoral scenes of Tir-Na-Nog and the human realm interspersed with portraits faerie folk and mortals; carvings only a master would attempt to create. The artistry looked familiar, but he couldn't place where he had seen such skill before.

They finally reached the bottom and walked down a tunnel dug from the earth, a series of thick roots laced themselves along the walls and the arching roof to secure it. The floor, a soft loam, was cool on Alex's paws, but soon gave way to a mosaic marbled tile and the ceiling expanded to three to four times the height of the tunnel. His nails clicked on the tile, expanding to thunderous echoes in the hall. In this space were several steaming pools. "T'is here I take my leave o' ye. Once ye've yer fill, ye'll be directed ta the hall above."

Cernunnos waved a hand in leaving, and Alex shifted back in his human form, naked, painfully erect, driven half mad as a stag at the beginning of rutting season.

Alex walked toward the pool and the water's surface of the nearest was broken by an emerging woman, followed by another, both naked. "Welcome, Hunter." He stopped mid-stride and he was painfully aware of his current condition. Their hair was braided and tied up at their napes so he could get an unobstructed view of their voluptuous bodies.

They sauntered toward him, rolling their hips to draw attention to the apex of their thighs. There was something vaguely familiar about their synchronized movements but his head was preoccupied with primal thoughts: Hunt, kill, eat, mate; he couldn't think beyond. The hunt had ended prematurely, and while he'd changed tactics and targeted prey before he didn't smell fear on them. Their pheromones wafted over his still-heightened predatory senses and a new need surged to the forefront.

"Hunter, we are gladdened by yer success and safe return." The dulcet tones slid over him followed by their hands on his chest.

The hunt over, the contest decided, it was his right and obligation as alpha, as all alphas before him, to set the hierarchical order within his pack. Instinct ruled. He heard the roar and the growl of conquest; it hammered at him with each beat of his heart. He was Hunter. He was home, finally, in the Wild Hunt.

He sank to his knees taking one of the women with him, the other circled behind trailing her fingers across his shoulders. "Dae ye require additional attendants?"

As he impaled himself deep within the first, he grunted with shock of sensation, but he turned his head to the source of the inquiry, "Aye, summon them."

Chapter 9

Brenawyn opened her eyes and sat up. "Oh, it's so late in the morning, why didn't you wake me?"

Alex handed her a bowl of oatmeal and berries. "Good morrow, lass. Break your fast wi' me?"

Brenawyn looked down at her state of dishabille and blushed, casting overt glances in turn at him and the tent, relative safety, several yards away.

"Brenawyn, there is no shame in what ye offered, what we did last night. But if you regret it, I ask for yer forgiveness. I'll turn my back." He put down the spoon, rose turning…

"No, Alex, please, that's not what I meant."

He turned back to find Brenawyn had closed the distance between them, the blanket and his plaid discarded on the ground on the other side of the campfire. She stood naked to the sky and his perusal. He opened his arms. "Careful, lass, ye doonae ken the forces ye play with. Say the word and I'll take ye again."

"Sounds good," she nuzzled him…

Brenawyn tried with all her might to hold onto the dream. She refused to open her eyes, and lay quietly in bed thinking about the kiss. Reaching under the covers, she found she was slick with need. Holding onto the memory of his hands, his mouth on her, his fingers, his cock in her—she found her release; but she wasn't sated. She needed him.

Biology, yes that was it, identifying the strongest and most virile man with wide shoulders, rippling muscles, not an ounce of spare flesh on him, no sign of a receding hairline, in fact no sign of a single gray hair in that luxurious dark silky head of hair. She sighed wistfully. He had the body of legend, honed not in gyms with modern-day weight equipment, but muscles hewn from demanding physical labor and intense weapon training—the body of a warrior.

Brenawyn pulled herself out of her medieval fantasy and into the very real medieval nightmare. She was astounded that the brief reprieve had allowed her to forget where and when she was. She'd slept like she had when she was a child, deeply and soundly. It probably had to do with that fact that there was no ambient light from alarm clocks, cell phones, street lights, and no sounds of passing traffic.

She was restless today. Days had crept by at a snail's pace and Brenawyn was feeling the need to be productive. Her pattern was to spend it primarily in the tower room reading from the limited selection in William's vast library. She wished that she'd had the forethought to take more than the requisite number of world language classes when she was in school. She would have loved to be able to read *The Divine*

Comedy in its original vernacular Italian. Even if she could, she didn't think she be able to settle enough to note the exiled author's nuanced allegorical rebuke of a corrupt institution.

Alex was in Tir-Na-Nog, safe, or that's what she was told, until she arrived before Samhain— Halloween—same date. It was September now. She didn't know how she would get there, how she would find him. It was curious that no one seemed to be concerned over that point except for her. She knew of no one who could help her. There was no one she could trust with the truth of her origins, and she had to keep out of sight from Liam and his wife and child. Not that she could do anything about it right at this moment being held prisoner so effectively. If she got away somehow, where would she go?

Then there was Maggie. She was in no position to help there either; she didn't even know where Cormac had taken her. Guilt washed over her. It was her fault that Maggie was mixed up with this mess. The decision to take up the mantle had been one made under duress. Tricked into it, she hadn't thought of the effects it would have on her loved ones.

Nana. She would have called the police to report Maggie's kidnapping. Perhaps all her worry was for naught because they could have already apprehended Cormac, and Maggie was safe. Brenawyn rocketed out of bed, her bare feet slapping the stone flags to pace.

She was impotent here. She couldn't call for an update. She couldn't coordinate a search party. She needed to get out of here!

If she had known that she'd end up here, a veritable prisoner in a time and place where danger lurked around every corner, as well as in the hearts of those that seemed kind, she would have reconsidered. Actually, she never would have promised anything in the first place if she'd known that her oath was built on empty promises, that she wasn't in fact ensuring Alex's survival. To hell with this whole thing!

She heard the grating of the key in the lock, but the door opened too quickly, giving Brenawyn almost no warning, and in blew Mistress Fordoun with an entourage of young strapping boys carrying buckets of steaming water. Even though Brenawyn was fully clothed, she had been there long enough to know she was in dishabille as evidenced by the appreciative side glances she received from the boys. She repositioned the screen and caught her reflection in the mirror, sleep tousled hair, rosy cheeks, and nipples straining against the soft lawn of the nightdress. Holy Lord, she was indecent!

The water brigade disbanded after the third visit, leaving a tub filled with lavender scented, steaming water. Mrs. Fordoun made efficient work of laying out a new dress and all of its sundry articles on the bed that had been newly made by one of the girls, as the other laid out breakfast. The smell of the pastries beckoned her, but as she approached, tea was poured, and at the smell Brenawyn's stomach heaved. She covered her mouth and made it just in time to the chamber pot to empty her stomach of last night's dinner.

"Och, are ye a'right, dearie?"

Wiping her mouth with the back of hand, Brenawyn pushed the pot away and looked at her reflection in the mirror. "Yes, I'll be right there." She felt her breasts. They were tender and sensitive. *No! This can't be.* She pulled taut the fabric against her abdomen and turned to look at her reflection in profile. She couldn't have children. Doctors—second and third opinions even—had told her that.

She'd had unprotected sex three times. Stupid. Stupid. The first time was…well, she didn't know how to categorize that. Imbued by spirits, she couldn't even bring herself to say it out loud because it made no flipping sense, but if anyone could say that they had no control over what happened it was her…somehow that seemed like a cop-out too. She was a responsible woman, and if she could remember the encounter, certainly she could have made sure that precautions were taken.

The second time was all her fault. Ill-advised certainly. She was scared. She needed reassurances. She needed something normal, and whatever else sex might be, it has a normalcy to it. She wasn't thinking with that encounter. Maybe it was a need to strengthen the attachment to the only person who knew what the hell was happening.

The third time was definitely that. She had vowed to accept the mantle of priestess, to forego all she knew, to leave her loved ones behind, and go keep the balance from a disintegrating covenant and assassination attempts by the Coven who wanted her power. She wanted sex from Alex. She used him to center herself, to feel the immediacy of the act and block out all else. It was a primal and pointed need of satiation and gratification, to serve and be served. The need made sense to her, the lust for his body, what it could do to hers, and how she responded. She had intentionally been reckless.

Pregnancy was not a possibility, or so she thought. She had only conceived the one time and then…the miscarriage and the doctors had told her there was too much scarring and trauma done to ever hope for another. There was a whole host of infections and diseases she could contract, too. Pus-filled images of infected sores from herpes, gonorrhea, and chlamydia floated to the surface of her mind burned there from high school health classes. Then there were scarier things like syphilis and HIV, without the presence of antibiotics in 1457, meant a prolonged and probably painful death.

Stupid.

But if he were here, she knew she'd want him to fuck her. She needed him inside her, filling her.

What the hell was wrong with her?

Brenawyn brushed the hair away from her face and stepped out from behind the screen. The tea and pastries had been taken away and what was left was a bowl of what looked like oatmeal, a hunk of bread, its crust crisp and flaky, a small round of cheese, and an earthenware pitcher.

Mistress Fordoun looked up after smoothing the bedcovers one last time. "Are ye sure yer a'right? I can send up a physic if ye ken t'will help."

"No, thank you, but could you tell me the date?"

"Oh!" Fordoun's eyes went directly to Brenawyn's abdomen, "t'is the eighteenth o' September, my lady."

Brenawyn must have made a small noise, because Fordoun flew over to help her to the edge of the bed. "Are yer courses late, then?"

As tears spilled over, Brenawyn only nodded, not trusting herself to speak.

"Och, lass, ye'll no' be the first woman who was brought ta tears o'er it, but I can tell ye from experience, havin' six o' my own living, that bairns are worth all the trouble and worry they cause. Ye'll see."

Brenawyn was in shock. A baby. Could she be pregnant? How did they tell here, besides the obvious? There was no early detection test that a woman could go purchase at the pharmacy. Did they just assume until it was beyond doubt?

And if she was? Not ideal circumstances, but a baby!

If she were home, she'd be able to support herself without a husband. She'd have to apply for a teaching job for the benefit of health insurance, paying for a college education eventually, and providing a financial future beyond what Liam's death benefit left her.

Shit, Liam.

He was alive and here. How would he react when he found out? She needed to get out of here immediately, before he came back. There was no telling his reaction. He left her and even faked his death, true, but coming face to face with her pregnancy by another man? He would not react well, just based on her own reaction to the news that he had a wife and child here. Having her mind cleared of the memory bindings just days ago, Brenawyn remembered every abuse, bruise, and broken bone, as if they had been just inflicted, but still, his domestic arrangement stung, and a small part of her, the part that was beaten in submission by an abusive man, thought herself undeserving and flawed to even have that.

She was in real danger here, and although she might not be able to assimilate to life here in the long term, submissive and dependent on a husband as expected of women in this time, she knew that she needed the protection of one now more than ever. She might make herself useful as a teacher, or work in the kitchen, gardens, or as a maid; but she couldn't support herself on her own. She'd have to live at the mercy of a man like William Sinclair if Alex didn't come back, and while William seemed to be compassionate to her plight; it wouldn't necessarily be the same with all the men in this Keep.

The magistrate, this Amergin, needed to get here now. The sooner he came, the sooner Brenawyn could leave with him. Once she did, the sooner she'd be able to think beyond the immediate.

Chapter 10

Maggie awoke to loud noises. The floorboards above groaned as heavy items were dragged across them, raining particles and imagined spiders unseated from their webs on her person. She sat up, but there was nowhere for her to go to escape the deluge. It stopped as soon as the cellar door swung open and something metal, by the sound of it, was dragged down the stairs. There were murmured curses, a fumbling, and a loud crash as whatever it was, was heaved the rest of the way. A second set of feet came rushing down as a result.

"How do you expect me to get her out of here if I don't bring her up in the wheelchair?"

"If you'd listen to me in the first place, and drug the bitch. It wouldn't be such a problem." This was a new voice.

"No, then she'd only be dead weight, and harder to bring up. Why were you so insistent that she'd be kept down here anyway? It's not as if she be able to escape with her leg the way it is."

"No, but she could have seen something to give her an advantage."

"Such as? There's no one around for miles. She could scream until she had no voice left for all the good it would do her."

"But to allow her to orient herself is advantage enough."

"Well, you would know being the expert on kidnapping."

"Damn, Andy, do you want me to call Cormac and let him deal with you and her?"

There was a sigh, "No, of course not, Linda. Please, let me handle this. Let me prove myself."

"All right, but Andy, don't disappoint him again. I'm getting tired of paying for your mistakes."

Maggie had to feign disinterest when Andy appeared at the door, luckily that wasn't too hard to do since the pain was still so acute. He left the wheelchair just beyond the opening since the doorway wouldn't allow for the width of the chair. "Hello, Maggie. It's time to go. Are you ready?"

"To get out of here? Yes. Where are you taking me?"

"Upstairs. That's all I know."

"All you know or all you're willing to share?" Maggie immediately regretted asking because the look he fired at her was daunting. Gone was the gawky awkward boy; this man was determined. He meant business.

He stalked over to her, grabbed her under the arms, and hoisted before she was ready. She collapsed into him and stumbled when he stepped away. He caught her and exhaled loudly, expressing his impatience, but he slowed nonetheless and started helping her to the wheelchair with a firm arm around her waist. It made him awkward since he was so much taller, so he stopped her to sweep her up in his arms and take her the last twenty feet to the doorjamb. He had to readjust, holding her closer to his body and walk through the door sideways to allow for the casted leg. He sat her down but stepped back quickly, running his hands through his hair as he paced away.

Maggie situated herself, sitting back more firmly for the ascent he'd soon make with her poised precariously on two wheels, completely helpless if he were to lose his grip. She'd fall and there would be little she could do to protect herself from further injury—best to make nice and appear helpless. He'd respond to that. She'd have to keep reminding herself of that, too. It was too easy for her to slip into sarcasm. It marked her personality, but it provoked him.

Andy circled back and took the handles without saying a word, and pushed her toward the stairs. Maggie didn't remember this part of the cellar because the only time she had passed through she had been drugged. It was expansive, much larger than the room in which she was kept. She could make out outlines of furniture under white tarps, piled like jigsaw puzzle pieces. There was a crystal chandeliers wrapped in clear plastic hanging off to the side on a hook. Neatly piled boxes with their contents listed in the same slanted print lined the far wall perpendicular to the stairs. The sight made Maggie think of curated museum storage or police evidence rooms, an image she must have gotten from a TV show or movie. She hadn't seen either of those places in person.

The stairs looked impossibly high, and she was grateful that she had been out of it when they brought her down. If she needed more confirmation that she was in an old house, the stairs offered it. The treads were short, the risers unevenly spaced, and there was no handrail. It wouldn't pass code now, so the house had to have been built in the 1800s or before. She had been in plenty of buildings built prior to 1700. As campy as the Salem tourist sites were, she'd liked to visit them, although foregoing if she could, the usual guided tours because they came with too many Blessed Be and So Mote It Be's. Actually, those came not from the guides but the fanatical patrons who didn't realize or care if they were being offensive. She wasn't offended really, not because of the religious bent anyway, god, with a capital G didn't exist, she had long ago decided, or if he did he was deaf to little girls' prayers. It really just bugged her that people were so fake.

At the base of the stairs Andy pivoted the chair and Maggie felt the back wheel hit the tread of the first stair. Stepping on the back, she was tilted so she looked up at Andy. From this inverted position he looked like a teenager again.

"Here we go. Stay still and don't worry. I won't let go."

Maggie nodded her head and closed her eyes. Maybe this way it would be over sooner. Closing her eyes didn't help though, the anxiety bubbled nonetheless and panic rose. She reached out to touch the wall; there was nothing she could hold onto, but she tried to employ the technique that her counselor once told her to identify things she could touch, see, and hear. If she could touch them, all the better. It grounded her. Andy grunted, "Keep your hands in." Maggie snatched her hands back, folding her arms and opting to bite her lip instead as she focused on her breathing and heartbeat.

Each thump of the wheels against the edge of the next step was another lump in her stomach. "You should have just sat me on the bottom and told me to pull myself up step by step on my ass. I do have one good leg and my arms work just fine."

"Not an option."

"No, really, we could still do that."

"No." Andy pulled harder, jostling Maggie in the chair so she had to grip the arm rests for security. "Can't have you relying on yourself to do things. Might give you ideas to do something foolish."

Maggie's mind worked. He wanted her completely dependent on him whether it was his wish, that bitch, Linda's, or Cormac's, the fucking bastard.

"It's either this way or being drugged again. Thought you'd prefer this way. It was not Linda's choice or Cormac's, though he doesn't bother with details. He'd opt for drugs because he doesn't want to be bothered with little issues. Remember why you are here. He is not a patient man."

Silence reigned except for a grunt and a thump with each stair until they reached the door. "Put your arms back and hook them around the door frame. You'll have to help with this last one. The frame is just wide enough for the chair and this last step is larger than the others. Ready?"

She was through the door and steered down the hall and into a front room. There were heavy brocade curtains drawn tight, their tasseled tiebacks hung open and empty at the sides. There was more furniture covered with the same tarps she'd seen downstairs, but this room had been used recently. There were a couple of rumpled tarp indents from people sitting on the couches and a trash bin overflowing with paper products and Styrofoam containers.

Andy stretched his arms, pulling from the elbow across his body and repeated it on the other side.

"I'm sorry I'm so heavy."

"Heavy? No. You're not fat. You could use a good sandwich or two in fact." He laughed, "Though that *would* have made my job harder. Seriously, though it was just awkward. Don't worry for me."

Linda, a heavy-set woman in her mid-thirties with stringy brown hair, came in the room with a cloth sack and zip ties. "The van's packed and pulled up out front. All we need to do is get her in it."

"Have you heard from Cormac?"

"He'll meet us at the destination."

"I see." Andy said reaching for the zip ties. He turned toward Maggie and held them up.

The first thought was to resist. It was bad for her if they moved her, less likely that she would be found. Linda must have seen the hesitation because she grabbed Maggie's wrist painfully and slapped her hard enough to taste blood. Linda was strong and she had both of her arms prisoner holding them out for Andy to tie.

"Make it tight."

"I am. It wouldn't do any of us any good if it cut off circulation."

"What do we care? She doesn't need her hands for what Cormac has in mind."

Maggie screamed and struggled.

"Hush," Andy said, "it'll be okay." As he bound her hands, he looked up. "Can I see you out in the hall, Linda?" His tone indicated that it wasn't a request.

Straightening her spine, Linda dropped the cloth sack over Maggie's head and tightened the drawstrings to fit snugly around her neck.

They didn't walk all that far because Maggie could still hear them clearly.

"What do you think you are doing scaring her like that?"

"Like what?"

"You know what! We have a long way to go—just us, undetected, because if we're caught, you and I will be going away for a long time. Do you think Cormac will help us? Think again, Linda. We need her calm and quiet."

"Not if she's drugged." Linda turned and before Andy could catch her, she was back in the room plunging the needle into Maggie's arm.

Disoriented because of the sack, it didn't register what had been done until Maggie started to drift out of consciousness.

Chapter 11

A chill was in the air when he awoke; but the breeze brought the smell of a doe with her fawn nearing the den—perhaps that was what woke him. The underlying obligation to make sure the pack had food to winter another year. The rest of the pack was sleeping still, nuzzled together with exception to the pup who stood precariously on the rump of another adult to chew on the Alpha's ear. He rolled, and the pup pounced, trying out his rudimentary training. The Alpha pawed at him, revealing his neck in another exercise to instruct on vulnerabilities. The pup, he knew, could sense it, just as he could, the soft, exposed weakness of the throat. The skin smelled different here. It was a beacon for determined fangs and unrelenting pressure to end a life. What was death to one meant life to more. To survive, to live, there was no difference.

The pup's tail wagged against the Alpha's chest indicating the loss of concentration. Whines and yips emanated from the pup, and for a moment the Alpha was content to play with this child—pup.

These fleeting moments were to be treasured, few and far between were the times when the entire pack ate their glut, where they all slept the sleep of the *sated. The Alpha was a good one. His pack was well fed. Luck had a lot to do with that. Most others felt the gnawing hunger most days, pups died, older members sacrificed themselves for the good of the group. Not in his pack, though.*

The sharp, needle teeth called the Alpha back to the present to find the pup pulling on a jowl. The Alpha raised a paw and swatted it to the ground. Last to go was his hold on his jowl. Enough. Once loose, the Alpha shook his great head smarting from the nips.

He rose and looked out over the pack in the darkened den. They were nuzzled together in a heap of grey fur, one indistinguishable from the next, and turned his attention to the doe and fawn. They were grazing closer now unaware of the wolves. He decided to let them be. This wasn't a decision based on mercy, but nature. The pack did not kill unless it was necessary. They didn't need to eat. Tomorrow, and all the days after, yes. The story might end differently if the two happened this way again, but for now he wished for the mother to teach her offspring what it was to be a deer, to show her the sweetness of new grass, to show her what it was to run in the open field.

It took a while for the Alex to realize he was awake. Bare arms and legs akimbo were too close to the nestled warmth of the dream. Alex squeezed a breast and patted a leg of another woman so he could get up. One hunger sated for the moment, now he needed food. He was hungrier than he ever remembered being in his life. His stomach felt empty and he smelled roasted meat coming from somewhere above. It called to him.

He left the sleeping women and wandered close to the cavernous walls. There, by another carved staircase was a stone table set into the wall. On it was a hunting kilt and belt. He swathed his hips, securing it at his waist and ascended to search out food.

Climbing, sounds of activity met his ears indiscernible at first, but the more he climbed the raucous laughter, music—*one of the stringed instruments was out of tune*—competed with each other; rather the troubadour's tenor was drowned amid the noise of inattentive guests. It was too bad, really, because he had a strong voice reaching ranges not often heard without strain.

He entered the hall from a side door, and saw the expansive room decorated with carved wood frescos covering the walls and ceiling, each depicting detailed scenes from a Hunt. The first among them, from before history began, was petrified Wattieza, the first tree, and its polished ebony grain shown as if it glowed from within. It had the place of honor, decorating the open dome above the circular dais in the the center of the room. The floors were covered in scenes, too, fashioned of stone mosaics. Polished semi-precious stones caught the vibrancy of the Hunting Grounds' flora and the vivid red of the kill.

He was drawn to a corner of the room to look at the newest addition, half completed. He recognized the wolves—himself leading them in semi-circle formation around Ruadan. The most striking element though wasn't the carvings' minute detail, *the fur of the wolves even looked soft*, but the wood itself. It wasn't cured, and sap ran freely from its pores over the figures and pooled in the fine lines blurring the features. He wondered the purpose of time wasted, of art destroyed, when a shadow fell over him.

Alex turned to see Pendragon with two goblets. He handed one to Alex and remarked, "Yer likeness is depicted hundreds o' times in this room, but this is the first as a Hunter and the one that drove the prey to ground no less."

"I didnae make the kill."

"Details...it nay matters. Yer first was a god. I doonae envy ye the enemy ye've made and the misery he will likely inflict upon yer person, but t'is a caveat."

"What is?"

"I ha' been a Hunter for near twice as long as ye've been a part of the Wild Hunt, and I've only claimed the capture once."

"I am painfully aware. I was there when it happened, aye?"

"Aye, hate me, but doonae begrudge me the acclaim I won that day."

"Yer point?"

"My point is that ye routed a full blood god on yer first go, and beyond yer temporary arrangement with Cernunnos, and I'm sure it doesnae feel temporary, but it is nonetheless, ye are a mortal."

"I'm sure ta be called again soon as I am free back ta the Grounds to be hunted by Ruadan—

Pendragon looked at him in disbelief, and put his hand on Alex's shoulder, "Ye doonae ken?"

Alex shook his head, "What?"

Pendragon leaned his head back and let out a guffaw. Once he settled down, he clapped Alex on the back, "Ye'll ne'er serve as prey again, as long as ye keep in good favor with Cernunnos."

Alex's heart leapt at the possibility for he thought he was fated to be the favored prey of the Hunt eternally. "But how? Why?"

"As ta that, I cannae say. The will o' the gods and all o' that, no' for mortals ta venture a guess. He'll tell ye in his time or no'. Come, enough talk. We feast!"

They approached two empty seats at the table, Edric was on the one side, and Cernunnos on the other. Before being given leave to take his seat by the god, Alex looked around at the table. Seated were all of the members of the day's hunting party and he wondered if this was everyone. Seen in this venue, the party seemed sparse, but their collective ferocity on the field was the tipping point, for each was lethal and merciless. Alex had direct knowledge of this, having been at the blade's edge of most of these competitors.

He died at their hands, and was brought back stronger, faster…more of an animal. How many resented the fact that they would never hunt him again? Or as frequently, he amended, sure that he'd anger Cernunnos sooner than later. He was prime, as elusive as the unicorn, as unique as the chimera with the magic of the warrior caste and shapeshifting abilities of the Reliquary. He'd made an enemy of Ruadan sure, but there was resentment simmering and future violence on the horizon.

Cernunnos nodded and indicated the seat next to him. "I'm sure ye doonae mind that we ha' started without ye, particularly since ye were otherwise engaged."

"Nay." A pinprick of trepidation flickered in Alex's mind at mention of his latest exploits, a thought immediately tramped down at the memory of eager hands and mouths and hot, slick cunts. He shifted in his seat, physically aware that he wasn't as sated as he had thought he was. Perhaps later he could find his way down there again.

At the nearest door a servant appeared and sharply clapped twice looking back through the door as a line of serving girls brought in larders full of meat. This first servant, a handsome woman with silvered hair, led the parade to the circular table and flipped a bare section of it up to allow the food servers passage.

"The table was modeled after one I had in my

home once. T'is terribly efficient, aye?"

Alex looked at Pendragon with a smirk, "Ye say ye had a round table?"

Pendragon looked perplexed. "Aye, I did just say that." He glanced at Edric on his left and the man just shrugged and grabbed for a turkey leg.

Alex was amused by the utter genius of the centuries' worth of poets that made a mundane object so renown. It was a table, nothing more.

Alex's mouth watered at the delicacies paraded before him. Haunches of beef, pork, lamb, turkey, and chicken; seafood in all forms: octopus, lobster, shrimp, salmon, tuna, swordfish, shark; his plate wasn't large enough. He ate with gusto and demanded more.

A different flank of serving girls made sure goblets were never empty. Reaching over shoulders, they rubbed against the party, some so emboldened as to push Alex's hands against their bosom or their sex. He could feel the heat of their core even through the overskirts. Many of the men took advantage of the offered flesh. A couple of the more courteous rose from the table with a maid or two to a distance not too far off, to dine in another way. Edric was not so gracious, swiping at the dishes before him. He placed a girl on the table; her skirts rucked up to her waist sitting in way that gave Alex a clear view of her pleasure.

There was depravity here and he sobered at the realization. All were engaged in some sort of sexual sport at this point, even Pendragon, though he had the respect to retire from the room. Alex saw him disappear with an auburn-haired beauty and suddenly wondered what Arthur's wife had looked like.

Alex got up from the chair and turned in Cernunnos' direction. He sat focused on his plate as he consumed food and wine, unconcerned about the orgy happening all around. There was a small contingent of serving girls flitting around him. They were attentive, to his dining needs solely. A few noticed Alex and they looked back and forth between the two, visibly hesitant at who to serve. Their problem was apparent, leave Cernunnos and run the chance with garnering his ire. Alex had been there plenty of times, not an area he'd wish on his enemy let alone women. Alex shook his head indicating he wanted nothing.

The true situation made itself clear in that moment when he saw relief reflected in their eyes. They were expected to please the members of the hunting party, and now that he was a part of that group—he felt nauseated. He grabbed for a goblet but the wine turned to vinegar in his mouth. He stuffed a forkful of pork in his mouth and it turned to ash. He was on the other side of the slave-master construct and all he felt now was shame.

Cernunnos looked askance at him. "Before ye leave this hall, ken that ye cannae return until the conclusion of the next Hunt, whenever that may be. If ye don't leave, however, ye can bask in all the delights that it has ta offer for as long as…"

"Understood, but I'm ready," Alex wanted nothing more than to run from these halls never to return.

Cernunnos wiped his mouth and hands on a folded cloth napkin provided by a serving girl, and waved away the basin of steaming water to rise from his chair. "Och, then a word 'afore ye go?"

Alex fell into pace with the god and soon found himself back in front of the half-finished fresco depicting his Hunt. "Dae ye like it?"

"Aye, t'is a rare artist ye ha' here. How many dae ye employ ta dae this?" He waved a hand indicating the entire structure.

"I didnae ken. Ne'er ha' given it thought. As with everything, it just is. Record 'afore there was history, record long after those who care are dust."

Alex nodded, but only because he couldn't think of anything to say in response. It spoke of grim fate and the useless struggle against the inevitable. He didn't need to be reminded.

After a moment Cernunnos sighed and touched the dripping sap, rubbing it between his fingers. "all o' the frescos ha' started the same, carved from unseasoned wood. The sap starts the alchemic process of turning wood ta stone."

"Takes an incredibly long time, in the mortal world."

"Even longer here." In an act that belied his soft

response, Cernunnos put his fist through the half-completed panel.

Alex reeled back from the sudden violence. All action in all corners of the room stopped and Alex felt the weight of stares at his back. When nothing else occurred, the sighs, moans, and rising slap of flesh on flesh rose again. This was his cue to leave.

"One additional thing, Reliquary." Cernunnos snapped his fingers to someone behind Alex, "Ken that I should just let be, but I owe ye for finding my daughter."

Three of the women he had serviced in the pools below arrived, nodded at some unspoken command, and all turned to Alex at once. The one nearest smiled and ran her hands over her face, over the top of her head, and down to her shoulders, her appearance changing as she did so. Blonde hair darkened to the blue black of a raven's wing. The next woman did the same. Her skin lightened and cheekbones lifted. And the third, her lips plumped and her eyes when she opened them were the color of new grass.

They were Dearg Due, cursed for ill-placed lasciviousness to forever be predators that fed on sexual desire. They were dangerous because they could sense the secret desires of their prey and could glamour into any form. Here they were, three of them in the same form of the woman he forgot.

Horror filled him as the last of the Wolf left his

mind clear. *Brenawyn.*

How could I forget?

The hands of all three went to their abdomen cradling a growing pregnancy.

I left her pregnant with my child.

How could I forget?

I'm not worthy of her affection. I vowed to protect her, took vows even if she never retuned my feelings, knowing the companion curse of the Dearg Due, that of the Gancanagh, would claim me.

How could I forget her?

I'm her protector, but I can't protect her from myself.

Chapter 12

Dressed and coiffed, Brenawyn was bustled out the door, escorted down to a private inner garden off the solar, and ordered to take several hours in the sun. Her familiar guard courteously stood barring the only entrance to the garden. Man of few words, he left her alone with her thoughts. Surrounded on four sides with stone walls, it did offer sanctuary from prying eyes and the sun was out, the first day since her arrival. The sun felt good on her face so Brenawyn couldn't even say she was put off by being ordered about so.

Her stomach did settle, and she felt better with the perceived freedom that the small excursion offered. She had paced the tower room and knew the diameter and circumference of it using her foot as a measure. Not one to suffer from claustrophobia, but the walls were closing in on her. The sky, the little that could be seen from the narrow windows, had a much greater effect on the muted colors of the stone greying them to match the dismal clouds.

Now that Brenawyn was out and the sun made its bashful appearance, she'd soak up what she could. She sat on a wooden bench with her back against a stone wall. The meticulous garden was tended by someone with an eye for horticultural landscaping. It wasn't that there was a lot of color, but the shades and textures of the various bushes, mosses, and ferns made it soothing and peaceful. The mature trees already heard the call of the coming winter with leaves painted colors of the sunset, half of which were scattered on the ground. There were vignettes of pruned shrubs planted in knot designs interspersed with plants that were familiar though she didn't know most of their names. She did see the dried seed heads of coneflowers, Brenawyn remembered reading somewhere that there was a medicinal purpose, though she didn't know what it was good for, how to prepare it, or even which part was useful. What good was she now? She lived in a time when all she needed was to go to the pharmacy to buy cold medicine.

The wind picked up, raising gooseflesh on Brenawyn's exposed skin and she regretted refusing the scarf, Mistress Fordoun called it a fechu, to cover the top of her chest. Other than that, though, the multi-layered skirt and the bodice protected her. Even though the sun was warm, it would soon be swallowed by the encroaching clouds, and with it the damp and rain would return. She could feel it in the air; it wouldn't be long before the cold settled in and heavier garments would have to be worn. Since she had been here, talk of the almost ever-present rain was a common topic of conversation; she must have heard dozens of words to refer to the rain: kaavie, bleeter, hagger, though now she couldn't remember the intensity of rain each described. She wondered if they had such a list for snow.

Where would she be when the weather turned? Brenawyn couldn't decide whether she wished for the magistrate to come so she could leave, or if she preferred that he stay away. It was solely the fear of the unknown with the first. It would be best if she left posthaste to get away from the immediate threat: Liam, his family, his friends. Movement would also appear like progress. She had to find Alex, but she didn't know if in her leaving she would be heading in the right direction. There was Maggie, too. Finding her, or at least information about her whereabouts, would probably be easier, although it depended on the bastard's motivation in abducting her.

Lost in thought, Brenawyn didn't hear him approach until he sat on the bench with her. She was startled as much by the quietude of his demeanor as by his sudden appearance. He didn't even look her way, just sat with his hands invisibly folded in the voluminous sleeves that his belted plaid created. He stared out into the garden without acknowledging her, and it was Brenawyn who scanned the area and saw several other unoccupied benches. It wasn't as if she felt that she had a right to the area, but the longer he sat there, the more she felt that he was intentionally encroaching upon her solitude. He could have sat at any other bench if he did not want to interact, but yet he sat next to her. He had a small thin frame, not more than 5'2 standing, but yet he was spreading out as men generally tended to do when relaxed, legs spread wide encroaching on her portion of the bench. When his knee touched her skirts, she turned to him.

"Good morning. My name is Brenawyn—

"Aye, mistress, the whole countryside is a chatter with news o' ye."

"Then you have me at a disadvantage."

He contemplated her, pressing his lips together in an exaggerated, comical way until Brenawyn realized he didn't have any front teeth.

He stood with some effort and faced her. He swept into a deep bow, elegant really, "I am Amergin Ambrosius, at yer service, my lady."

"Oh, you're the magistrate. I've been waiting for you."

"Ah, if that were only true," he laughed deeply. "T'is been some time since a lass as bonny as ye has waited for me."

Brenawyn felt color creep into her cheeks.

"Here for less than a fortnight, and makin' trouble for Himself from the outset. Are ye daft, hmm?" He grabbed her chin and forced her face up, pushing his own to stare into her eyes. "If no' for Sinclair, ye might ha' been ash by now. T'is sore dangerous ta declare yerself now. No tolerance, no exception. A witch ye'd be, and they'd suffer not a witch ta live." He let go and patted her head as if she were a child.

"There ha' been so many poor souls that were condemned without one ounce o' proof and gone the way o' the flame, and then ye come. What possessed ye woman, ta show yer magic?"

Brenawyn stammered. "I um…I didn't know. Um…I…can you help me?"

He clapped his hands and rubbed them together vigorously. He was a few feet away but Brenawyn could feel the heat generated by the action. One moment his hands were empty, then the next they were cupped, light shining from between his fingers. He opened his hands and a ball of blue flame sat in his palms. "Aye, my lady, as o' right this moment, I am the only one who can help ye."

"How much danger am I in?"

"We cannae be too careful. We will ha' ta bide for a few more days here. Mistress Fordoun can see yer outfitted proper for our journey and I need ta access my library, consulting my scrolls, then we can depart. Three days, I am thinking."

~~~

Brenawyn was in the eye of the storm that was Mistress Fordoun. The minute the travel plans were announced, she went into a flurry of preparations, and God help the man, woman, or child who got in her way, she'd wrangle them into helping.

In the matter of two days, Mistress Fordoun oversaw the creation of a whole fashion line, the amassing of cooking and medicinal supplies, a small crop of various fruits and vegetables, and had say in the stoutness of the pack horses that would be supplied. In this time, Amergin was nowhere to be found, though to go anywhere in the Keep was to hear stories of his exploits and those of his ancestors of the same appellation.

This night's dinner was no different with a jaunty melody filling Hall. The raucous laughter and merriment died as everyone became riveted on the troubadour singing of Amergin's ancestor of the same name, fooling the Formorians and Tuatha Dé alike.

Brenawyn ate her fill, and then some more, before she pushed back from the table trying in vain to find more breathing room. Her stomach hurt from being so full. She thought back to when she had overeaten when she was home, and the waistline of her pants seemed like a dream compared to the stricture of the corset. How did women bear it?

"Are ye enjoying the entertainment, my lady?"

Brenawyn turned to William . "Yes, I am."

"Good, good. Afterward, I'd like ta invite ye ta my solar. I ha' a few items that I would like ye ta relay ta my brother if ye see him. I'm thinking that ye will ha' a better chance than I would at that."

"Certainly."

He stood and offered his arm. "Shall we?"

Brenawyn wiped her mouth with the cloth napkin and stood. Absent was her constant guard, she noticed,

The Oracle's Curse 107

THE ORACLE'S CURSE 107

but she was otherwise unconcerned.

When he opened the door, Dunmor nosed and whined his way to Brenawyn. She knelt down and buried her face in his ruff, scratching him on both sides of his barrel chest. "And I'll miss you most of all."

Sinclair navigated around them and reached his desk. By the time he'd retrieved the bound package, she was in the room sitting in one of the chairs by the fire, barely discernable due to the mass of writhing fur that concurrently panted and wiggled to get closer to her. "Och, down, boy!" Swatting at empty air to show the dog he meant business. "He is besotted with ye."

"He's a good boy. Reminds me a lot of my dog, Spencer. I miss him so."

Sinclair nodded and handed her the packet. "It's mostly, a set of letters informing Alex of the Keep's goings on, how people are, ye ken. There's an inquiry that he particularly needs ta see if ye get a chance, tell him that it requires his immediate attention."

"All right, I will remember to tell him if I see him, but…

"Aye?"

"Um…I don't know where he is, or where I'm going at that. You might be better off sending someone else to find him."

"I ken where he is, but no' how ta get there. Ta send someone ta seek it out means that he would ne'er find it. Or if by chance, he did, t'would be on the sheer chance that a faerie's interest was piqued. Ta send someone ta the nearest faerie hill, would be scouting madness. Inta the realm o' the gods no mortal should go."

"So you have some idea where he is?"

"Tir-Na-Nog at best, but the Hunting Grounds most probably."

"Then you see my dilemma. I have made an impossible promise…"

"I ken o' impossible promises, indirectly at least. I ken the turmoil and heartbreak they cause. Mourning a life lost ta ye, but not in the usual way. Ta always be separated by a great divide that cannae be surmounted and then havin' those around ye be suffering the same. He's dead officially, dae ye ken that? I ha' hope that one day I will get ta see him again, but with each passing year," he sighed, "the grey is in my hair, and my joints ache. How much longer will I live?"

"I'm sorry for your loss. And more importantly, for any involvement I may have had or will have in your continued separation."

Sinclair looked at her considering, "E'en though I am not gifted the way Alex is, I dae ken the gods, and involvement with their machinations is ne'er simple, so I simply thank you for yer thoughtfulness. What impossible promise did they manage out o' ye?"

"Two, in fact. I blindly agreed to take up the mantle of high priestess, the one that had been prophesied."

He gasped.

"What?"

Sinclair shook his head, waving away concern, "Are ye daft then?"

"Hey, it was under duress. I found out afterward that *your* brother was in no danger of dying anyway! But it was too late then to rescind a promise." Brenawyn crossed her arms.

"Aye, I am that sorry, I am, but did ye no' ken the type o' trickery when dealing with the faerie?"

"No, I did not, but ignorance is no defense."

Sinclair sat back in his chair, "I suppose no'. Go on, then."

"Alex is with Cernunnos being housed in Tir-Na-Nog until I find my way there before Halloween—Samhain. I got the god to promise not to make him run the course until then, but it's just a stay of execution, I'm thinking. Right?"

"Aye. Ye are quite the pair." Sinclair got up to retrieve two goblets, and poured claret into each.

"No, thank you," she said, but he pressed it into her hand.

"Since ye are the priestess now regardless if t'is only in name, ye'll ha' ta preside o'er the fire feasts, Samhain being the next. During the feasts the veil is thinnest 'tween realms. Ye willnae ha' ta go in search o' it. Where'er ye are, the gods will come ta ye, and thus show ye by their arrival the gateway. If Alex is with Cernunnos he'll show too."

"I'm glad, but that sounds too easy."

Sinclair laughed heartily, which put Brenawyn at ease. "Amergin is planning on taking ye ta Anglesey—Bryn Celli Ddu, ta be exact. Be wary, my lady, Amergin is the only other I would trust ye ta for yer safe keeping, beyond my brother, but make no mistake, his presence will rouse the ire o' the Tuatha Dé and the Formorians both."

"Because of his ancestor's pretense in the Accords? Seems awfully petty for so long ago."

"The faerie are petty, true, but as ta his ancestor?" He shook his head, "It was Amergin himself who tricked the gods."

"What? How is that possible? How many years ago was that?"

He held up his glass to her, "A topic for yer journey."

What did she remember from Finvarra's story in the caverns? Nuada, Balor, Bres and the Battles of Magh Tuireadh—war and political intrigue and then a no-name comes on the scene and fools them all. She'd be walking into a powder keg set to blow.

Chapter 13

Maggie didn't remember the ride to their new destination nor the vehicle itself, though that was probably for the best. She had once traveled via ambulance a few years ago strapped to a stretcher, and she remembered being worn out from the ride. Her muscles, particularly her abdominals, ached from the constant tensing in response to the fear of rolling off the stretcher, even though that wasn't possible. Fighting to keep her balance while drugged was probably not good for her anxiety. She needed her wits about her so she needed to avoid disorientation and that meant drug induced stupors.

She was in the dark, quite literally, but it was dry, and there was a concrete floor. There was a dripping faucet somewhere in the vicinity but that told her nothing. She had to wait until someone showed up.

She must have drifted off to sleep again because the next time she woke it was too bright lights. Covering her eyes from the fluorescent overheads, she realized she was in a large storage room. Metal shelves lined the longest walls, packed with cleaning supplies and boxes. Three people entered: Andy, Linda, and some other man Maggie hadn't seen before. They rushed her. Hands rucked up her skirt past her waist, and Maggie panicked. Linda slapped at her hands pulling them up over her head.

"Shh. It's okay." Andy soothed, pulling the hem down to cover her nakedness, a little too slowly in Maggie's estimation. "We have to get your cast off. There's someone here that can see to your healing, but the cast needs to come off first."

At his word a cast cutter made its appearance, operated by the new guy who avoided her eyes. A formidable looking tool, but she knew that the blade wouldn't cut her skin. She tensed anyway, and was immediately punished by pain from the break. *Did they keep her drugged for longer than the transit? What happened to hasten the timeline? Or was this the plan all long and the cast just temporary insurance that she didn't injure herself further?*

The cutter made quick work of the cast and it was off without too much pain. The real shock was the temperature change; it raised goosebumps.

"Do you have an immobilizer? Or is the healer on premises already?"

A brace materialized and was handed to him. It was new, and he ripped open the plastic bag, laying the brace on the floor next to Maggie. "Where are the pins for the hinges?"

A quick search revealed that they were on the brace itself attached to one of the hinges. He fumbled with the small plastic pieces; one fell through his fingers and rolled under the next shelf. "No, don't," he said as Andy knelt to retrieve it. "They have extra." He picked up the brace and snapped them into place one after another. "She won't be able to bend her leg and you'll have to be cautious; take extra care when moving her. It won't hold her leg as well as the cast."

He positioned the brace, and Andy was there holding her ankle and lifting, putting a supporting had under her thigh. "Take a deep breath, it will be over soon."

The man slid the brace under and Andy gently put her leg back down.

The man sat back on his heels looking down at Maggie's leg. "I can't secure the main strap because it would be directly over her stitches. The leg shouldn't even have been cast in the first place because of them." He took hold of her leg and pressed around the stitches making Maggie hiss through her teeth.

"Hush, girl." It was the first time he addressed her, but his eyes still didn't meet hers.

"There's no sign of infection. Are you still feeding her antibiotics?"

Andy responded, "Yes, she still has a couple of days left on the second round of them. We've been giving her injections twice a day.

Second round…if the same length of time still held true, one round of antibiotics for something like this was ten days, then the second minus a few days; she's been gone for almost three weeks! Factoring in the change of locations once in an indeterminate direction and distance, her chances of being found were almost nonexistent.

The man nodded and stood, wiping at his knees. "My suggestion is that you keep her drugged until the healer comes. It would lessen the chances of her moving and make your job of supervision easier."

Andy stuck out his hand, "We'll take that under advisement." The man looked at it, scowled, and turned to walk away. Andy looked down at Maggie for an instant with his arm still foolishly extended. He looked vulnerable for that instant, and Maggie reached out to touch his ankle. He looked down at her, frowning. His hand at first went to his side, and despite the hardening of his features, and perhaps it was because of her touch, he immediately brought his hands up and raked his fingers through his hair.

He grunted and stalked out of the room leaving Maggie with Linda. She was quick about her duties, bedpan first, then instructed Maggie to make use of the newly filled wash basin, drink, and eat; Maggie did as told. Then the before mentioned injections: antibiotic and sedative, had Maggie drifting off before she had put her head down again.

Maggie woke sometime later to find the overheard fluorescents on and Andy sitting on the other side of the room reading a book. "Sleep well?"

Maggie opened her hands and looked around, not bothering to answer him.

"You've had the last dose of antibiotics and no more sedatives before the healer comes. Apparently, you have to be awake and sedative free for him to do what he does."

"I've seen healers at work. That part makes sense from what I've observed."

"I never have seen a healer work. What was it like?"

"An extreme case, he was dead."

"Dead? Like as in dead, dead?"

"Yup. There was no doubt."

"No way! That can't be."

"It's the truth. Multiple stab wounds and he was gutted."

"Get the hell out of here!"

"Wish that I could. Have you ever seen an animal gutted?"

"Can't say that I have."

"One of my mother's boyfriends was a hunter. Took me along when I was twelve. We sat in a tree blind for days it seemed before a stag wandered in. The deer was impossibly thin, I didn't think it was a good choice being so thin. What did I know?" Maggie shrugged her shoulders and looked up at the ceiling for a long moment before continuing. "He told me that it was the end of rutting season, and stags don't stop to eat, the instinct to mate overrides all others. The asshole was a good shot at least, one arrow from his crossbow killed it. He strung it up and wrapped my hand around the handle of his knife covering it with his own and gutted the deer. All of its insides fell out. There was so much there, hardly seemed like it all could have fit inside. That was the way for Al—the man."

"What did the healer do first?"

Maggie laughed sardonically, "What do you think? She scooped up the entrails and shoved them back in, then sewed up the abdomen."

"Holy shit, that must have been something to see."

"Oh yeah, sure, after I vomited from the sight, I don't know how I was able to thread needles for the stitches. I know I threw up afterward too."

"Did you know him?"

Maggie looked at him, lips tight, and shook her head unwilling to continue the conversation. "How long was I out for?"

"Two days. We put a catheter in."

Maggie lifted the blankets, and gasped. "I'm never getting out of here, am I?"

"Relax. It was just temporary." He got up from his chair and placed the book face down on the seat. Turning to her again, "I could take it out now if you'd like."

"No! Don't come near me!"

Andy stepped back holding his hands up. "You need to relax. Who do you think undressed you in the basement? Moved you from there to here? Attended to your needs while you were sedated?"

"Didn't give it too much thought, but it wouldn't have been Cormac. It's beneath him to do so, and Linda, for that matter, resents me or the idea of babysitting. Since you and Linda have been here since the beginning it's either or both of you. Then of course, you're asking stupid leading questions now, so my guess is you."

"Exactly." He came over and squatted down near her. "If I wanted to take advantage, I would have already."

"A gentleman and a kidnapper. You are quite the hero."

Andy sighed, "It's the best you are going to get. I'm sorry. We all have our roles to play. Don't hate me because this is yours."

"I don't, not at all." She tore off the blankets and hiked up the skirt of her dress and laid back down turning her head to the wall. "I hate you because *you* chose to play your role."

Chapter 14

Alex sat across from Cernunnos, a chess board in between them. A goblet of ambrosia sat next to him untouched.

Cernunnos cleared his throat, causing Alex to look up. "Time passes differently here, but it does pass."

Alex smiled and moved his bishop to a4.

"Yer head t'is no' in the game, Reliquary," as he moved his pawn resulting in a Bad Bishop. "Something on yer mind? Check in two."

Alex laid down his king. "Aye, preoccupied. Thinking on the priestess."

"Doonae be worrit. Amergin is with her now. They'll be leaving yer brother's keep ta journey to Bryn Celli Ddu on the morrow."

"Early, is it no?"

"For the Rite. Aye. T'will be less than a fortnight's travel, but methinks he means ta instruct her along the way."

Alex sighed, "A task for her protector." He surged to his feet and grabbed the goblet, downing the ambrosia in one swig. "I should be there, but I'm stuck here playing games with you."

"Dae I detect a note o' cynicism? Not a good stratagem ta curry favor from yer god. T'is yer luck that I am in a forgiving mood. E'en though I canna send ye back, lessons can be learned. Ye need ta pass the time. Study. Ye ha' access ta my libraries if ye wish it. May I suggest *The Art of War* by Sun Tzu?

"Reading…ye?"

Cernunnos gave him a withering look.

"That didnae come out the way I meant it. T'is just that reading is so inefficient, so time consuming for one such as ye. Ye can glean the meaning in more effectual ways."

"T'is truth what ye say, but," he smiled looking through Alex, "someone once showed me the pleasures o' it, and since then I indulge, partly as a way o' honoring she who showed me."

"Brenawyn will like that. She's a teacher—tutor rather."

"Dae ye think so? I admit that I'd no' given thought ta the aftermath o' her discovery. I wonder what she learned in her own studies. Nimue, yer mother, informed me that she doesnae ha' languages. Easily rectified, but t'is disconcerting. How does she communicate?"

"Things are different, times ha' changed. Ye'd ken this if ye spent any time in the mortal realm. Not just any time either, her time, that's important, ye ken? May I suggest that ye dae that 'afore she comes o' her own accord? Depending on yer motivation o' course, if ye expect ta ha' a relationship with her."

"My motivations are none o' yer concern."

"Granted." Alex held up his hands, "but knowing might make ye understand her better."

"Carrying yer progeny will delay bringing her here. I understand that mortal gestation is a delicate time. I will thus wait until she births yer son."

Alex stopped his pacing, pride swelling, "My son?" *My son. My boy.* Then guilt barged in. He'd forgotten her. Forgotten that she was carrying his child. He was unfaithful, a rutting beast, incensed with the need to copulate, to spill his seed into any willing cunt—would do so again and again when the beast next arose. How could she return his love once she found out what he truly was? And even if she did he wouldn't be able to be with her. He'd never be able to be the man she needed. He would be ashamed. He was ashamed. He wouldn't be able to go to her in faith, look her in the eye, and expose himself and all his foibles knowing he was unworthy. He didn't even know how he'd next handle seeing her.

He knew the cultural context of monogamy, though it was not one that he was raised with. Druids saw sexual congress through a different lens, but even in his culture, it was not uncommon, later in life for a man and woman to only seek out each other. If he was just a man, there wouldn't be a question. He had burned for her solely, long before he had taken the vow, the same that would make him Gancanagh. He was the Reliquary, and if that were it solely, he'd be able to manage it on the requisite days of celebration. She was the high priestess no less. The gods would turn their eyes from their raw emotion, but they would not be offended.

Brenawyn saw with her own eyes his cockstand after his shifting back from Wolf, even if she had no cause to think of the ramifications of it. That obstacle was manageable; no worse than the biological need to copulate after the fight or flight response. But his new, unwitting promotion from prey to hunter in the Wild Hunt was too elemental, too bound in the balance, to fight against. He was only mortal, and he hated the acknowledgement of his limitations. It was an excuse for bad behavior. He was no better than his students rationalizing their lewdness with the similar ideology as its human nature to cheat.

When Brenawyn did not return his feelings, he'd eventually become the monster, in truth, that he was already ashamed of being. His future as a gancanagh, the male version of the dearg due, an incubus feeding on the sexual desires of women where their every orgasm he brought them to would take them one step closer to addiction. Once there it would be a breathless promise cried out during climax to push them over to an eternity as a dearg due. Would he care?

Pulling himself out of his reflection, "The priestess will be almost four months along by Samhain. T'is nay wonder that her powers are developing exponentially. She'll need ta be protected from the Coven until her safe delivery, else they'll get the idea ta use her for their own purposes." Alex continued, "Afterward, the boy will need protection, if what ye ha' in mind for her takes her away from her mothering duties."

"Doonae presume ye are the only one ta best protect either o' them. T'is solely the flaw o' arrogance that makes ye kin that ye are meant for her. As for the boy, ye only supplied the seed o' what's ta come. Doonae get attached, down that road only heartache lives. But as for protection until her safe delivery, I ha' heard, and grant ye leave ta do what ye can ta insure the safety o' the priestess and her child. We will attend the Rite, and afterward ye may stay ta protect them."

Alex bowed low, "I thank ye, my lord."

Chapter 15

Riding a horse in the countryside was a pastoral fantasy next to the reality of the slow-moving, muscle-cramping, monotony that Brenawyn was currently in. She envied the others in the group who looked like they were born on the back of a horse. This was no relatively flat, well-worn trail led by a guide as her mount followed the lead horse in the Watchung Nature Preserve. Here there were hills, unremarkable she thought, if she were walking, but mounted she felt like if she didn't grip the saddle with her thigh muscles, she'd go tumbling off head first. She was having involuntary muscle spasms, a new, alarming development. She had thought she was in shape after spending years on the elliptical and taking Pilates classes only to find that there were new ways her muscles could be worked.

She wasn't a novice rider, but this was no steeplechase. She had taken some beginning classes when she was a teenager, but lost interest the first time she was thrown from a horse. His name was Blueberry, but Lucifer was more apt she thought, as she remembered him now. He was on the smallish side, a mottled grey almost blue in certain lights—hence his name. But he was the most cantankerous horse, she'd ever seen in her life. She'd been bitten by him more than once. The instructor's idea was for the horses to get accustomed to their new riders, and every time she approached him with apples in her hand, he'd opt to try to take a bite out of her instead. It didn't make one bit of sense because she was always tall, certainly the tallest in the group but she was always given the smallest horse—Blueberry. She'd beg her father to get her there early, and vie for Bailey, a lovely chestnut mare who loved to be brushed on the neck and withers. She'd muck her stall, bring new hay, and saddle her; but the instructor always gave her Blueberry.

Brenawyn had this daydream of galloping across the fields, her hair blown back by the wind that the episodes with Blueberry never quite crushed. Now, riding this amiable animal, another idyllic daydream was squashed. It didn't surprise her other than to note how unprepared for life here she was.

She was cranky, trying unsuccessfully to shift once again, stuffing her skirts under her posterior to give some cushion to the growing blisters that were sure to be forming. "When are we stopping for the night?"

Amergin sighed, "That is the sixth time ye've asked that question in the past hour."

"I'm sorry. I have no sense of direction." This last was true enough, but her sense of distance was off, too. She was told that the trip would take just ten days. How far could the horses go in a day's travel? Twenty, thirty miles before they were overtaxed? Three hundred miles would be an afternoon in a car. She missed slipping behind the wheel of her car and hearing the throaty, hungry sound it made when she started its 470-hp 6.4-liter V8. She didn't have to look at the tachometer; she'd know by the feel of the gears that it was time to shift. It was too much car—was told so mostly by men—but what the hell did they know? She was too dainty, too pretty, perhaps a Volkswagen would suit her better? She scoffed aloud at the memory. Sure thing, right down to its little bud vase on the dash. She should get something with better gas mileage her teacher friends would tell her. No. She was attracted to the power, and considering everything, it was a safe avenue. Even with the memory bindings in place, she had to know on some unconscious level, and if that were true, perhaps what they said about men and sports cars was true in some regard with her. She was trying to prove something.

She reached out to pat the neck of her mount. She chortled, horse power indeed, of one, and as long as she kept the apples coming beyond resting and watering, he'd be responsive.

The gentle nature of her mount and his plodding along, however jauntily, was not going to be enough to keep her mind off her body aches. She turned to Amergin. "Where's our first stop?"

"Tonight? A place called Melrose Abbey."

"An abbey? Is that wise? William was concerned about the bishop arriving before you did."

"Aye, t'is a concern, surely, but we'll ha' ta chance it. There are those there that I trust. Despite what ye may ken about us, there are those that are learned and not so easily given ta hysterics o' witchcraft."

"But, you're not concerned for yourself?"

"Och, no. I am a crotchety wee bastart most o' the time, but when I want ta be I still ha' me charms and I can play the game. Ye're a different matter altogether, though. Yer smart, that's for sure, and yer bonny and that might get ye out o' some entanglements, but the moment ye open yer mouth, ye've announced ye're a foreigner and thereby suspect."

Brenawyn frowned.

"That might be overlooked, but the wide-eyed look that ye ha' it just declares ye as a member o' the faerie folk."

"What? You don't believe that!"

"Nay, no' I, but the way ye look at everyday things…t'is with an interest that belies logic. E'en though there are many who doonae believe, no' so much time has passed that the stories are all forgotten. They're still exist mostly ta scare children ta behave, but in all tales o' faerie folk who cross the veil, they are full o' wonder and mischief at what this realm holds. Ye ha' that look about ye. T'is no' me that ye ha' ta convince either; and I wasnae there when ye appeared in the glen, my lady. T'is obvious that ye come from...*elsewhere*. Ye've heard what they call ye?"

She nodded, realizing the enormity of her situation. "I wasn't allowed to wander the Keep. The day that you found me in William's garden was the only time I was given to be alone with my thoughts. I was escorted to Hall for dinner and then back again to the tower. On two occasions I was taken to the solar. When was it do you think that people were able to observe me being...I don't know, odd?"

"Dinner is a very telling time, I've found. People are pre-occupied with eating; they lower their guard. It allows for a rather uninterrupted view. I ha' been observing ye from the first."

"Really? That's a bit unnerving, and pray tell what did you observe? Any secret cackling, evil-eye giving moments that you caught?"

Amergin glowered at Brenawyn. "Doonae be a petulant child, and doonae jest about the evil-eye. Say that ta the wrong man and ye'll be arrested and burned 'afore ye ken it."

She made a distraught sound stopping Amergin's chastisement. He sidled his horse up to her, patting her on the shoulder. "There, there. T'will be a'right. Ye willnae go the way o' the flame, naught if I ha' any say about it."

Brenawyn scoffed, "That's very comforting."

"T'is the time we live in. Think back if ye will. Can ye tell me what overall feeling ye had from the crowd gathered for the meal?"

She considered. The Hall was loud with the bustle of people. Servants ran to and fro with trays laden with food and drink intent on filling larders and pint glasses. It was also loud with a multitude of conversations and the music from the dais. She didn't think anyone paid her any mind, so intent they were on the food in front of them or the conversation at hand. No one had bothered to engage with her. They were tired and dirty, often stretching to ease their aching joints. They didn't look about. And that's what Amergin was speaking of. She did gawk at everything, so thrilled that she was witness to an actual medieval Hall. She wasn't bone-tired as everyone else was from hard labor, but she showed wide-eyed enthusiasm that trumped any exhaustion.

Amergin nodded as she relayed her observations.

"So, what do I do?"

"Ye ha' no choice but ta trust that I will keep ye safe. At some point, we may ha' ta break with the guard. Two can escape notice much better than a dozen armed mounted men and their contingent. We just need ta get ta Melrose so I can meet my contact. Afterward I'll ha' a better bead on what awaits us."

"And this conversation—a measure of my fortitude?"

He chuckled, "Fortitude is measured, in truth, by

adversity. That has no' shown its face as o' yet." He looked through his bushy eyebrows at her, "It will 'afore long, mind ye." He clicked his tongue and rode ahead leaving her to contemplate the weight of his words.

Left alone in her solitude surrounded at a distance by the rest of the party, half the Keep's garrison it seemed, it was awhile before Brenawyn thought to match the gait of Amergin's horse, and once done they rode in silence for a bit longer. She broke the silence asking, "Do you know when the transition in belief came about?"

"T'was in increments. Invasion is violent and that is what is remembered; but true conquest is insidious, an act accomplished by gradual assimilation once everything seems ta ha' returned ta normalcy. It worms its way into the hearths and hearts slowly starting on the outskirts with a promise o' hope and help. This one was an easy step, too; many o' the tenets were similar: the Triple Mother was replaced by the Trinity, the Wheel of Time replaced by Days of Obligation, fire feasts replaced by High Holy Days.

I say, go inta any kirk, and look at their idols— Christian and Druid mixed ye'd find. Christ and the Green Man—Cernunnos himself, being carved at this very moment for the chapel in Sinclair's Keep. I ken why, I doonae blame him. He is a man who kens the truth and has ta play the game, too. It doesnae e'en matter much where his beliefs lie. I cannae blame any o' them, except for the hypocrites. Sinclair has seen too much ta disavow loyalties. He's no' one o' those—those that say they are devout, but hide in fear, or worse use fear mongering ta incite others ta rash actions."

"So, what news are you expecting from your contact?"

"They will ha' been made aware o' the arrival o' the bishop for one, and might ha' an inkling o' how far afield the story o' ye traveled. There e'en might be word o' yer husband…"

"Not my husband!"

"I am sairy, my lady, my apologies, truly; but that wee bastart has made himself scarce since Sinclair sent him off."

"You don't trust him?"

"Sinclair claims that he's *his* man, but I *ken* him. He is too ambitious, too eager ta breach the veil. He's no' gifted enough ta succeed, but that makes him dangerous for he's willing ta gamble. T'is no' the last time we'll see him."

Amergin pivoted in his saddle and shielded his eyes from the glare of the sun through the clouds. He cupped his mouth and made a series of sharp pitched sounds much like the bird calls she had been hearing from the brush. A responding call was heard from far afield, and he turned to her and squeezed her hand smiling. He kicked his horse into a canter and wheeled around to find the captain of the guard behind them.

After brief instructions with Amergin doing all the talking and the guard just nodding his head in her direction, Brenawyn saw Amergin head off across the field at a gallop, hunched low against the horse, and the captain, the same guard who was charged with watching her in the Keep surge up to meet her. "Well met, my lady."

"Good afternoon. Are you to keep me company then?"

"Aye, my lady, until the Myrddin returns." He turned and in response Brenawyn's horse followed suit. "We are ta await him elsewhere."

"Has our destination changed?"

"For the now. I hope it willnae cause ye undue strain ta make camp in the woods. The Myrddin thinks it wise ta avoid the Abbey."

"Whatever you think best. Lead on." Brenawyn absentmindedly fidgeted in the saddle, rubbing her posterior as she looked over her shoulder in the direction of Amergin's departure. She wondered what the change was: was it the bishop or Liam? Hysterical mob with pitchforks and torches? Witch hunters?

It was hours of plodding along in a different trajectory before they stopped. By then Brenawyn had to ask for help in dismounting but she still wound up in a crumpled heap practically under her horse that nosed her with interest, probably to see if she had any more apples. The animal's velvety lips tickled her neck and the horse whinnied in response to her giggle.

Camp was made efficiently around her. Her horse was led away with the rest a short distance off, and she found her way to an empty boulder next to a young man pulling string from his sporran.

Brenawyn announced her presence, "Hello there," waving stupidly. "May I sit with you?"

The young man smiled in return, and moved over clearing most of the boulder.

"What are you doing?"

"Getting ready ta set some snares since we'll be sleeping wild tonight."

"Mistress Fordoun packed enough to feed an army."

"Aye, that she does, bless her heart. Always looking out for us, she is. The provisions she's packed though are meant ta supplement with whate'er we hunt on the road." He picked up his knife and started carving a notch in a fallen branch.

"What can you catch with this type of snare?"

"Rabbits mostly, or similarly sized animals. Don't have much meat on them, but they make a soup taste better." He pointed to several other men around the perimeter with the hilt of his knife. "They're doing the same. With any luck, we'll ha' rabbit ta supplement our breakfast. Why don't ye go and see if ye can get something ta eat? T'will be a long night and there's a chill in the air."

Brenawyn wandered over and caught the eye of the only other woman in the group. The woman waved her over and offered her a bannock smeared with honey. Brenawyn accepted it with thanks, and stuffed it into her mouth in response to the rumbling in her stomach. It was fresh and heavenly and tasted like more.

"T'is good, aye? Freshly made this morning, they were, and packed while they were still hot. Though," she lowered her voice as if the mistress were amongst the company and could overhear, "when they are stale, ye'd ha' a time getting them down yer gullet with a whole flask o' ale."

Brenawyn choked on her last bite, and then recovering, "I'll keep that in mind."

"I am Isla, ye ken my husband, Tavish." She pointed to the captain of the guards.

"Oh, he never told me his name," even though Brenawyn had asked on several occasions. "Pleased to meet you, Isla," as she extended her hand.

She looked at Brenawyn's hand, and closed it with her own giving a familiar pat. "I apologize for me thick-heided clout o' a husband," shaking her head, "they doonae think that something as simple as a name would be useful. Can ye imagine, callin' them all by, 'Hey, ye!'" Tavish turned toward her, and she laughed turning her back to him dismissing him out of turn, "Aye, I'm speakin' ta ye, ye ol' bampot," she said, rolling her eyes.

Brenawyn laughed. "They are certainly single-minded at times, but as the saying goes, you can't live with them, and you can't live without them."

She sighed, "Aye, that's the truth o' it. So I am ta serve as yer lady in waiting."

"What? I don't need…"

"Oh, d' ye ha' a way ta get in and out o' yer stays then? Of course we'd ha' ta be in an inn for that ta actually matter. Sleeping with the night's sky as yer blanket, ye need ta be ready if anything were ta happen. T'is only good sense ta dae so."

"Under those circumstances, I thank you then."

Isla nodded her head and handed her a blanket roll. "Come we'd best find our rest while it's still ta be had."

Brenawyn woke some time later to the soft snoring of Isla next to her. The fire had died down to embers and there were shadows of two guards keeping watch. She recognized one as the snare man she spoke to earlier. She heard soft nickers of the horses and the light clinking of their harnesses. The rest of the company was identifiable as blanketed lumps sparsely positioned around her, instead of the fire. Their placement seemed strategic but the why of it slipped from her mind.

She rose to her feet wrapping her shawl tight around her shoulders. It had come loose in her slumber and just as predicted, there was a chill in the air that made gooseflesh rise on her arms. It wasn't cold enough to see her breath, but she could smell the promise of it on the air.

Brenawyn carefully chose her path to the trees beyond to relieve herself. The guard nodded to her pulling at his forelock as she passed. She held her skirts as she stepped into the underbrush, and lurched in, blinded by both darkness and foliage as to where she was stepping. There was no way she would make a good hunter. Every cracked branch and crushed leaf echoed around her announcing her position. Any animal would have scampered away at her first footfall, so she was utterly surprised to find a stag facing her when she rounded a tree.

She stood still, trying to think of what a survivalist guide would say about wild animal contact. It was a buck, but she had seen Animals Gone Wild, *even laughed at the predicaments that dumbasses got themselves into, and here she was facing down one with twelve points. Gored by buck was not the way she wanted to go regardless of the time she was in.*

The buck sniffed the air and took a step toward her, nose flaring to get her scent. The action reminded her of Spencer. It was close enough that she could see by light of the full moon the little wrinkles on the bridge of its snout as he assessed. She missed her dog. How many times in the past weeks could she have used his canine comfort?

The buck was close enough now that she could reach out and touch it, but her hands stayed at her side. It was the buck that closed the distance, nosing her like her horse, then it licked the back of her hand.

Brenawyn let out her breath that she hadn't realized she was holding and put a tentative hand up closed like how she was taught to approach an unfamiliar dog. Seeing no aggression, she opened her hand and touched its head between the antlers, and the buck leaned into her caress turning its head almost to give her better access. "Itchy, are you?" The buck mewed, and its back leg spasmed. "Oh, I see I got a spot." She laughed, "Does that feel good, puppy?"

The breeze sighed, "Priestess."

She jumped back, her spine plastered to the tree behind her and she whipped her head looking around for the source of the intrusion.

"Relax. Doonae be frightened."

Brenawyn gasped when she found the voice's source was directly in front of her. "No, no, no!" Hands cupping her ears, "You are not supposed to talk."

"Priestess, ye're dreamin'"

"No, no, no!"

"Touch the tree. Dae it. Just touch the tree."

Without opening her eyes, she splayed her hand against the trunk she was leaning against.

"Ye need ta look, my lady, ta see the truth in what I say."

She opened one eye, and looked down. The trunk was undulating under her hand. It was solid against her back, but liquid mercury under her fingers.

"Believe me now?"

"I've...I've seen this before."

"Aye, in Tir-Na-Nog. This is no' that. T'is yer dreaming self, I ha' no real power ta change much in another's dreams. Just enough ta convince ye mayhap?"

"Amergin? Is that you?"

The buck lowered his head giving a good rendition of a formal bow complete with the leg extension. "T'is me a' yer service."

"But how?"

"One of my abilities, t'is no' complicated. I could teach ye ta dae it in an afternoon. The connection was made when ye touched the buck."

"Are you telling me that we initiated a fucking mind meld? My mind to your mind and all of that?"

"I doonae ken what ye are referring ta and I suggest ye hold yer whist. There's things that I need ta tell ye."

Brenawyn bent low to look directly into the buck's eyes.

"Lass, I wouldnae suggest ye do that. I doonae ha' complete control o' the beast. Ye're challenging him."

That sobered her and she stood taking a step back.

"There's a matter ta which I must attend. Ye are ta go with Tavish. He'll bring ye ta Bryn Celli Ddu. I've already instructed him. I will join ye again as soon as I may. Be safe."

The stag turned to go, but Brenawyn called out, "But what do I..."

"Go back, priestess, lay down on yer bedroll and awake for certain. All has been arranged. Be safe."

Chapter 16

It was a couple of days, at least that was what it seemed, before Maggie noticed any break in the routine of her guard. Her leg still hurt like hell and since there was no painkiller that she was being fed, she was acutely aware of it. She lost all modesty and didn't fuss when Andy touched her to tend to her hygienic needs. She didn't know how long she had been here, but before long, he'd have to deal with another of her needs. Good, she hoped her period would bring friends. Perhaps at that point he'd foist off responsibility on Linda. It served them both right.

The door burst open, scaring Maggie and Andy, too, who was sitting by the door reading.

"He's arrived. Come, Cormac wants us to greet him."

Andy tossed his book on the ground and stood, taking a tentative step in Linda's direction, then stopped. He regarded Maggie, and looked as if he were going to say something. She waited, but he turned from her and disappeared.

It was some time before Maggie heard the deadbolt release and the door open. Andy, Linda, and a figure cloaked in so much fabric she couldn't tell gender or age entered. A gnarled hand appeared, and

Maggie heart raced. Visions of the old woman in Leo's shop and again in the forest rose in her mind, even though she'd seen that bitch die. Nothing about this was rational. She could have been resurrected, right? Alex was, and Maggie had been a part of that. If he could be, why couldn't others?

The hooded person spoke. "Leave us."

Not the woman. A man. An old man. Someone new. She relaxed, as strange as it sounded; at least it wasn't the devil she knew.

Linda grabbed Andy's arm and towed him out of the room, closing the door behind them. The hooded man grabbed the chair and pulled it, metal legs squeaking across the floor to rest in the center of the room well out of arms reach from Maggie, and sat down facing her. "When ye are accustomed, we shall begin."

He stretched his legs out in front of him, crossing them at the ankles. His arms disappeared in the wide sleeves of his robe. The majority of his face was still in deep shadow, all she could see were the deep wrinkles of his lips and around his mouth evidence of someone missing most of his teeth, and sparse, grizzled whiskers covering his chin and lower jowls. A soft snore rose in moments, causing Maggie to raise her eyebrows.

She cleared her throat, impatient to get this over with. When he looked up, yawning, she could feel her ire rising. She indicated her wounded leg with exaggerated eye rolling.

He knelt as one much younger and clucked, looking at the damage to her leg. "Hurts, does it no'?"

She nodded trying to stretch out to get away from the pain.

He placed a light hand on her thigh, "All will be well shortly." He gasped and grabbed Maggie's chin to force her to look him in the eye. He took off the hood and leaned close, "Tell me lass, do ye ken the priestess? Brenawyn McAllister, she calls herself, though no' McAllister any longer."

Maggie tried to sit up. "Brenawyn? You've seen her? How is she? Is she home?"

"Aye, she is well, out o' her...*element*, but whole."

He sat back on his heels, staring at the wall chewing his lower lip.

"Get me out of here, please. Take me to her."

"Och, nay. Ye'll ha' ta bide. Ye'll see her 'afore long though. Then I'll be in a better position ta help both o' ye."

He looked at the Velcro fastening of the splint and he grabbed the end to pull it back. *Brrrrup.* His eyebrows shot up. "Ooh. That's fancy." He touched the fuzzy side, then the hook examining each closely, closing it again, just to rip it open. "O' all the ingenious things!"

"Can we hurry this along?"

"Och, aye, I suppose we must. Someone will come 'afore long." He pulled the splint out from underneath her leg and cast it aside gently. He put his hands on her leg, covering the stitches in their entirety and she felt his hands warm. The warmth spread to her skin. It felt hot, hotter than the blood underneath. Her leg flushed and swelled. Bruising appeared and expanded. Her leg swelled further. She cried out in panic, but was immediately hushed by the old man. "I need ta bring the blood ta the surface ta prompt accelerated healing. It willnae get more uncomfortable than this."

At his word, the pressure lessened. She felt the blood recede and looked down to see the bruising fade, from dark purple, to blue, to yellow, signs of healing. He took his hands away and she was shocked to see the presence of new skin, red and shiny, but whole. The fragments of suture thread hung in pieces that she brushed off. She ran her hands over clear skin; what was once a mass of contusions and a jagged line of stitch work showed no evidence of trauma.

She lightly pressed, no pain.

She moved her leg, no pain.

She persisted. "It doesn't hurt at all."

The old man nodded his head, "That's the idea," and smiled. "Listen closely, because we doonae ha' long. Keep yer head down, listen ta instructions, and doonae use yer sarcasm, if ye want ta live through this. I must go."

"Please don't leave me!" Maggie pleaded.

"Aye, I must, for now. I am nay use ta ye here. I doonae ken the field as o' yet nor who the key players are." He patted her hand, "Bide, lassie. Follow my direction. Ye'll be safe enough for now."

Chapter 17

Brenawyn awoke to mumbled conversation near her head. She opened her eyes to see Tavish bend to brush Isla's hair away from her face and give her a kiss on the forehead. Neither of them took any notice of her. "Lass, I'm going ta check the traps I placed, call out if ye need me. I willnae be far."

She heard Isla sigh as she laid back down, arm pillowing her head, back turned toward her, and a stockinged foot sticking out of the twisted blankets. She wondered how long they had been married. Catching a glimpse of the red and green plaid after he had disappeared in the tree line, Brenawyn couldn't hear his footfalls despite the thick layer of leaves and brush on the ground. Now there was a hunter.

What more would constitute a good husband here? Protection—most of which implied physical brawn and intent, ability to provide food—constant attention to animal tracks, making, laying, and checking of traps, hunting larger game and the danger that lay within, then gutting, skinning, and preservation of meat. There was no partnership equality, she knew, but seeing it for herself, how could there be? Even in the best circumstances, these people were eeking out a life for themselves despite almost insurmountable odds.

Clearly defined gender roles, something a modern-day woman would scoff at with cries ringing to the hilltops of sex discrimination, but what choice did they have here? Things had to get done. Harvesting, candle-making, baking, dying fabric, sewing, had to be done, too. It was eye-opening to see that this issue wasn't as black and white as it seemed sitting in twenty-first century society where most things were manufactured and as long as one had enough money or credit, they could purchase said items.

Brenawyn was soft and unfit for life here. Little good would her contemporary thought do her when she couldn't pull her share of the weight. She knew nothing of gathering and straining honey—which would keep for long periods of time without refrigeration, the making candles, milking a cow, or making butter. She knew how to cook and bake, that was something, but the ingredients didn't materialize out of a five-pound sack of all-purpose flour, already sifted three times. She thought she remembered reading that oats and barley were the predominant grain in the area, but how to harvest, mill, and grind the grain was lost on her.

A drop in temperature and increase of rainfall a couple of hundred years before made more land unproductive. Inhabitants would have had to make their farms self-sufficient in their production of meat, dairy, grain so they banded together. She saw this reflected in the community. Hunting would call the men away for periods of time. Protection, and a variety of other things that Brenawyn hadn't even thought of, would be the reason for further absences.

She was surprised with her knowledge of the time period, thanking whatever it was that made her focus on background information to teaching literature. Her students would bellyache about the purpose of knowing such drivel. If they only knew!

The fire was smoored sometime in the early night, but now there was some man attending to it, feeding it kindling to get it going again. Brenawyn's stomach rumbled and Isla turned over. "Sleep well?"

"Yes, all things considered." Brenawyn answered thinking back to her dream conversation with Amergin, but she sat up and dug at a rock in the soil, throwing it away in disgust and rubbing the small of her back.

"With any luck, we'll ha' fresh rabbit ta break our fast this morn. Tavish went ta walk the trap line."

Isla got to her feet and brushed her skirts. "Come, my lady, we'll go take a keek if there are mushrooms ta be had. Let me get my basket."

They walked in silence, Isla doing all the work, because Brenawyn knew what a dandelion was, and a coneflower, but not too much else. It would speak volumes against her if she picked something that was poisonous. Isla didn't notice or was too polite to comment but she was amiable company, and of the group Brenawyn felt the least nervous that she'd slip and reveal too much around her. It was probably the micro-focus on those gender roles that took the scary stuff off the table.

"Oh, chanterelles!" Isla scurried over to the tree beyond.

"How can you…"

She held a bright yellow specimen up for Brenawyn's inspection.

"Oh, I've never seen one that color before."

"They are good with cooked with venison, rabbit, or even squirrel if needs be. Come, help me. Look around. Gather them in yer apron; I've only the one basket. Mistress Fordoun will be much pleased by the gift, I tell ye."

Now that Brenawyn knew what to look for, the yellow of the chanterelles stuck out, whereas before they blended into the spectrum of foliage greens. They shared the space at the trunk's base with the soft green moss. Kneeling down to pick the first batch she'd noted the similarity in hue, yellow and green blended together from a distance. She brushed the velvety moss and she imagined Alex over her, inside her, on moss just like this. It seemed so long ago but that was only because so much had happened since; it was, in truth, only weeks ago.

She wandered, thinking that if she still heard the camp she was within calling. She became so absorbed in her task that she didn't notice when that wasn't the case. Thinking she traveled in a straight line, she tried to backtrack, but neither camp nor Isla came into sight. She retraced her steps and looked for the spots she'd disturbed picking the fungi. She found those immediately but was turned around, there was no way for her to tell which she had picked last. She felt she was going in circles.

"Isla!" she called. The noise disturbed a covey of grouse to her left and startled Brenawyn. Clutching her chest, she called again, "Isla, can you hear me?"

She tied the ends of her apron up into her waistband, a feat in itself because she had to dig under the bodice to fashion an impromptu sack for the mushrooms. She called again, cupping her hands around her mouth. "Isla!" But there was no response.

"Hello, Brenawyn."

She'd know that intonation anywhere. She spun on her heel to face Liam, armed to the teeth.

"What are you doing here? Didn't William send you away?"

"Aye, that he did."

"Knock off the accent, Liam. You never had one when we were together."

He nodded in acquiescence, "I've been waiting for you."

She backed up slowly, a useless reaction because she knew she had nowhere to go. He'd overtake her in mere seconds hindered and restricted by her garments as she was. "What do you want?"

He smiled, "You." Brenawyn's heart leapt at the proclamation, and then she remembered. His smile was his lure. It was same smile bestowed on her the night they met, the same smile when he broke her collarbone, the same he gave her right before he kicked her and she fell down the stairs.

"You can't have me."

"Untrue. We are no longer in your time. Here, you are my property to do with as I wish."

"But you told a hall full of people, your people I guess, since you came back here after… that you wanted rid of me."

"And that was true enough at the time, but you are a means to an end, *wife*. If only your ability had manifested then. We could have skipped all of this."

"And what pray tell was that? Faking your death? The memory bindings? The abuse?" With each question, Brenawyn's voiced grew louder until she "Our son?"

He looked up at that.

"Oh, you didn't know."

His voice cracked, "No. I did not. They didn't tell me."

"Well, it would have been hard to, wouldn't it have, since you left me to drive myself to the hospital. Do you know I only made it to the car, fainted behind the wheel from the pain, and the VanBrussels found me," she ranted, "and called an ambulance?"

He paced, and Brenawyn took several more steps back.

"Did you ever care about me at all?"

"You weren't hard to live with. Generous, considerate. There were many times I had to remind myself that…"

She put her hands on her waist, "Hmm?"

"That you were an assignment."

She scoffed, "An assignment."

"There were a number of potentials and I was given you."

"Don't bother to explain. I met Cormac. He explained it all very clearly." Brenawyn said the disdain dripping from her words.

Liam took exception to this and declared, "Cormac MacBrehon is going to be a god!"

"And what? Take you along with him? Don't be so naïve, Liam. There's no room at the top with him."

"You know nothing…" He stopped mid-sentence, and waved at her middle. "Take that ridiculous apron off. You look pregnant."

Brenawyn smirked, and untied the apron and the mushrooms tumbled out. She pressed the fabric tight across her abdomen. "Funny that you should say that. It's really too bad that you can't see through all these clothes." She turned in profile to him, "I've just started to…"

He was on her before she finished her sentence,

his hands around her throat. "You whore! Whose is it?" Pushing her back into a tree.

She was immediately sorry. Sorry that she'd provoked him. She knew what his reaction would be, but she did it anyway. He was dangerous, a loose cannon, and the decision to add fuel to the fire was already made. If she couldn't hurt him, she could make him angry.

"Alex."

His hold tightened; Brenawyn clawed at his hands. Blood rose to her face. Eyes bulged. Tongue protruded. He was going to kill her. Here. Now; 600 years in the past.

"I'm sorry," she managed to wheeze out. She saw spots. It was getter darker.

A large hand grasped his shoulder, but she couldn't see who it was. Then his hands were off her neck, she crumbled to the bracken choking as air filled her lungs. She felt a sharp pain to the back of her head, and then nothing.

~ ~ ~

Isla heard Brenawyn's raised voice a distance off. She put the basket down and crept along in the direction of the strammash, not recognizing the other voice speaking with the same discordant accent as the lady. Her instincts told her that Brenawyn was in trouble but having no inkling as to the breadth of it, Isla couldn't abandon her to get help. Right now,

Brenawyn's sole help lay in her, even if she were only there to witness it. She'd at least have something to report back to Tavish with.

He was going ta be hoppin' mad and had every right to be. He didn't say that she wasn't to take her gathering, but there was no use trying to take that course of reasoning with him. It was implied, and she very well knew it. He took his job seriously; his tasks each received his full attention. She knew that while he told her that he was going to check the traps he was also patrolling the perimeter looking for signs they were being followed. With any luck he had already come upon the ruffian's trail and was in pursuit.

She was now on her belly inching forward taking cover behind the ferns. She undid the knot and pulled her shawl up over her head to hide the blonde of her hair, making sure the fabric billowed out to hide the white of her blouse. The drab colors blended in with her surroundings and she was as concealed as she could be. She could see the man—Liam McAllister, though it confused her to hear him speak in this manner. It was stilted and awkward; she didn't know why he would speak thus.

She had been there in the Hall the night that Brenawyn was introduced by Himself. Her appearance was not such a shock, there were travelers that came on a regular basis, the Keep was along a well-traveled road. It wasn't a shock either, at least to her, that Brenawyn was introduced as the Sleeping Lady. She had been raised with the stories. Her granny told them well up until her last breath on this earth. Isla was over fond of them, and wished they were true. It was exciting to have one of them be real.

What was truly scandalous was standing next to Liam's wife, Colleen, and hearing her gasp, holding a hand to her mouth, tears streaming, when Liam proclaimed this new woman as his wife! Isla would never have pegged him as a lecher, an adulterer. He was always kind to her, charming and protective in a strictly appropriate way. He was a trusted man in a time when trust, even among family members, was dear. And then to hear him say that he wanted rid of this new woman. She didn't hear much after that, her attention was diverted by Colleen's swoon.

While it was true that no one knew what went on between a man and woman in the privacy of their own home, she heard Brenawyn accused him of memory bindings and faking his death. This was not something most people had to deal with. What was a memory binding anyway?

Brenawyn was inching back to where Isla lay. Perhaps, she could, with any luck, be a distraction. Tavish would not like one bit her putting herself in harm's way, but she had a sense of what was at stake—not that he confided in her ever. His manly sense of obligation would just have to take the insult and as a result she would most likely see the business end of his belt. She couldn't just sit back and do nothing—not when she felt responsible.

Isla got to her feet as Liam put his hands on Brenawyn's throat. Brenawyn's back was to her, and Liam was incensed, his only focus was in choking the life out of her. Brenawyn struggled, her body lifted until she stood on her toes. He was propelling her backward to the next tree, Isla's tree. The time to strike was now, picking up a tree branch, Isla brandished it like a club. But then there was a hand at her mouth, and an arm around her waist, she dropped the branch in her surprise, and windmilled her legs. She found purchase on the tree, the same which, on the other side Brenawyn was being choked. Isla pushed off, causing her captor to reel back and lose his balance. She rolled off him and swiped under her skirt for the paring knife she held in her garter, thinking of it just now. It wasn't meant for defense, its purpose was cutting vegetables, taking trimmings, but it was sharp, and would do in close quarters.

The man in question was robed in a voluminous grey, a match for the one Liam wore, a deep cowl covering his head. She pounced on him wielding her knife, pressing it to his throat, she pulled back the hood, and was met with the familiar face of one of her husband's guardsmen. She released pressure, certain that she was safe and had misread the situation, but he surged up to meet her, pining her arms to her side, his eyes glowing an incandescent red. She head-butted him, breaking his nose, and shoved the knife in his neck. Blood gushed from the nose, but little from the knife wound. He clawed at her still, a wiry strength still in evidence, and decided. She twisted the knife. Now there was blood—plenty of it. He gurgled and spasmed under her, mimicking the act of carnality.

Isla was shaking now, never having killed before. What if she'd misread the situation? That he didn't mean any mischief? That he was just trying to keep her quiet so he could get her out?

Desperate, breathless, end-of-life choking sounds brought her back to the present. Isla got to her feet, not thinking, but someone new snatched her hair painfully propelling her forward. He held her at arm's length and his grasped the roots at the base of her skull, so she couldn't turn. They rounded the tree, and she saw the light go out in Brenawyn's eyes, as the man behind her grabbed Liam's shoulder.

"T'is enough. We'll take both o' them. We cannae leave her behind."

"Kill her."

"And make her death the reason for Tavish's holy war against us? Nay. If she's no' here then there will be cause ta track us. In that time we'll be away."

"He'll follow."

"Aye. That he will, but he is a calculating man."

"Formidable."

"Predictable. Ye doonae want ta see someone like him when he thinks he's got nothing ta lose."

Chapter 18

Brenawyn awoke to find herself gagged and hog-tied, jostling along in the back of a covered wagon filled with rotting hay. It was night, but she could see the forms of two hooded men on horses bringing up the rear. Her restraints were tight, whoever had tied them knew what they were doing, and the knots were probably similarly set. While she could not possibly stand, she was able to shift positions and that was when she felt behind her and found another set of hands, likewise bound.

She moved enough to turn and saw the back of Isla's head.

She grunted through the gag. No response. She grunted again, louder this time. No response. Isla's hands were still warm and pliant so at least she was alive. Brenawyn rolled on her hands and her legs hit into the prone form of the woman, waking her with a start.

Isla struggled and emitted a gagging sound trying to rid herself of the cloth stuffed in her mouth. Brenawyn tried to ease her panic but only succeeded in leaning against the woman's back hoping to convey calm. It worked, and in moments Brenawyn felt her relax.

A bit more struggle and Isla was facing her in the tight enclosure. They were a little worse for wear, but whole, and all they could do was wait.

Brenawyn stopped fighting the movement of the cart and laid her head back down; she was much more comfortable though each bump in the road sent a painful shot of pins and needles down the arm and leg she was lying on. Her shoulder hurt from being kept in that position, and her legs cramped.

Isla fared no better.

The wagon came to an eventual stop and one of the hooded men climbed in toting a knife in his teeth. He hooked his arm behind Brenawyn's knees and yank her to the edge of the cart bed. She grunted as she received yet another jolt of pain from her bound extremities.

"Change o' plan, whore, we must depart the road now, and if ye give us any trouble, t'is yer companion that will feel the pain. Dae ye understand my meaning?"

Brenawyn nodded understanding, and the man sawed at the ropes behind her. The relief she felt when the fibers gave way was short-lived. Her legs couldn't hold her weight and she went crashing to the ground, grunting as new waves of pain wracked her body.

"If ye no' shut yer gob I'll tie ye back up."

She nodded as she sat up stretching her legs in

front of her, massaging the muscles to aid in relief with one hand while trying to free her mouth with the other. She managed to get the cloth out of her mouth, but it hung around her neck. She could breath, but the absence of the gag made her gulp in air. *They haven't killed me, so there must be a reason they're keeping me alive.*

Another guard was stationed to watch Brenawyn, and Isla was brought out and released from her bonds. Isla was not so subdued though; she sprang up as soon as she was freed, causing the original guard to tackle her to the ground. Brenawyn moved to help but her guard clamped an arm around her waist and a hand over her mouth. She bit him and tasted blood before he snatched back his hand, clouting her on the head enough for her vision to swim. The guard across the way clamped onto Isla's thigh and forced them open underneath him. The tone of Isla's grunts changed to panic as she tried desperately to get away from him.

Brenawyn saw this as the precursor to rape and her blood boiled. Her interlace flared to life and the ground shook. Liam came around the wagon on horseback and called for a cease. The trees beyond uprooted, and a deep crevice was forming in the midst of the road. Liam jumped down, paying Brenawyn no mind, and grabbed the man's cowl and tore it back. A knife appeared in his hand and he sliced through the man's carotid artery bathing Isla in his blood. He threw the man's convulsing form at an angle away from the woman and helped her up. Only then did he turn his attention to Brenawyn.

"She's safe. She's whole. Stand down or I will kill her right now."

Brenawyn had limited control over her powers. In the handful of times she'd used them only twice had she invoked their aid purposely. The first was to help revive Alex under the guidance of her grandmother, so that wasn't useful now. Nana wasn't here to guide her through mediation to accelerate the process of calming her emotions. The second though, what had she done? She was in the hall about to be formally presented publically so sanctuary could be granted and she brushed the child in passing. She felt the child's difficulty and knew what was wrong before she looked down. That was healing, her intuitive response through a projected offense, but this was defensive. It felt as if the magic came from a different place. She was angry and frightened as she had been in her grandmother's house after Cormac gutted Alex. She didn't understand it at the time, but the effect of causing the beams to crack was a physical one. Her muscles strained as the wood snapped but it wasn't the source of the magic then. It felt as if it originated in her gut because the moment's relief afterward was a visceral one. It made no sense, because it also felt like the source was her thinking—that she had to find a way out of that room somehow. Exiting through the downstairs store via the front stairs was blocked by Cormac. The body of Alex and the Oracle stood in the way of her escape down the back stairs. Her powers were tied to her emotions obviously, but she couldn't pinpoint what their source was.

She gained her feet, the crevice becoming wider, zigzagging its way to the fallen man, who was gone now, the last of his heart's blood seeped into the hardened earth. She didn't hear Liam, so intent on her ire, but when the body of the would-be perpetrator sunk into the earth, her anger leveled. With a wave of her hand, the banks of the crevice crashed in on each other with a muffled *whoosh.* Gone was any remnant of the guard.

Liam looked at the point where he had been and smiled. "I say again, stand down, priestess. You may be able to counter me before I kill her, but you will not be able to do anything for Leoncha or…Maggie."

At the name Brenawyn snapped out of her trance interlace becoming brighter, "You know where she is?"

"I know where she'll be. If I don't make it to our destination, she'll be dead."

"You're lying."

"Perhaps, but there's no way to tell. Stand down."

The wind was taken out of Brenawyn's sails, and she slumped, her interlace fading.

~ ~ ~

Tavish returned to camp with six hares cleaned

and already gutted; no use in attracting unwanted wildlife by the stink of offal. His stomach growled in anticipation of breakfast, but his wife was nowhere to be seen. He gave the job over to a junior member of his guard, silently swearing because the meat would be charred beyond recognition and barely be edible.

Where was that woman? He shouldn't be surprised, trouble seemed to find her. If he didn't know her better, he'd think she courted it. But truth be told, she was just naïve and gullible. Still, a sinking feeling settled in his gut. He should have been more specific. He should have told her to stay put. Where was Brenawyn? He shook his head, chastising himself for overlooking the obvious. He was better than that. Isla's confounded basket was missing. They were off together gathering herbs.

He sighed and left to track them down. He caught their trail immediately upon entering the tree line, thanks to the soft loam of the forest floor. It was easy to follow once he found the first tree, its soil disturbed at its base. He crouched down pinching the dirt to rub between his fingers. He smelled it, and detected a slight fruity scent. *Ah, its mushrooms, she's after.* They'd be close, roaming, looking for more. He scouted beyond and chose a direction.

He located several more sites, but neither Isla nor Brenawyn. He whistled, knowing the sound would travel farther. She'd hear it and backtrack, meeting somewhere in between. It didn't even occur to him that they could have separated, or never had been together in the first place, when he came upon her basket overturned, its yellow mushrooms scattered in a wide arc. She'd tossed it down.

He took a guess that Isla was following Brenawyn. There was no additional track, only his wife's small foot, the sharp indent evident of new shoes directly from the cobbler before they left. They were his gift to her to replace the much repaired old boots she had.

Where did she go? He paced the area before seeing the retreating footsteps. The footfalls were different, more determined, heavier on the heel. He followed the prints as they zigzagged from tree to tree almost as if she were using them for cover. She'd stopped here. Tavish looked around, scanning the area. Two trees beyond he saw crushed foliage. She'd taken to her belly. Whatever had taken place it had been close to have her taking further cover.

He came to the next tree and saw evidence of a struggle. She'd gotten up, was forced up—there was too much disturbed ground to imagine otherwise. He backed up and looked at the site through squinted eyes, trying to block out all else other than the clues: uprooted saplings, and an unearthed rock. Tavish touched the empty space the rock previously occupied. Small indents, her fingers, prying it out to use as a weapon. On the trunk of the birch there was an area chest high where the bark had been ripped off; dirt marked the exposed wood. Could that have been her?

He looked back. A body lay amidst the bracken. He went to investigate, pulling the hood back—it was Duncan, his guardsman with his wife's paring knife sticking out of his throat!

Tavish sat back on his haunches. Duncan was trusted, but as the body lay here, dressed an unfamiliar robe much like the one Amergin wore, it pointed to deceit.

He reenacted the scene from the clues. If this was she, Duncan towered over her. She'd know that she'd need to use momentum to her advantage. He'd had taught her that. She was petite, but agile. He'd taught her how to defend herself. If she was taken, and she was, who was he fooling? She'd not have gone without a fight. He rounded the tree and located another bunch of spilled mushrooms. There was another set of footprints, larger but still dainty. They must belong to Brenawyn. Then two larger sets. One matched the tracks beyond, the owner walked with a limp. The left foot fell awkwardly, heavier. He'd slow them down. That was important.

Having made mental notes of the rest, Tavish marked the tree with a swift swipe of his blade, and ran back to the camp calling for arms.

Chapter 19

Amergin opted to step through the veil into Tir-Na-Nog instead of performing the Rite of Widdershins. He normally liked to keep a low profile, erring on the side of caution, for it was far better to go unnoticed than to broadcast his comings and goings to the gods, But the Coven was emboldened by the looming possibilities that the coming fire feast offered. He needed to confer with Oghma, the God of Communication.

His intent and purpose must have preceded him because the god was quietly waiting for him when he turned from sealing his passage.

"Greetings to you, Myrddin. How do you fare?"

No matter how many years passed, Amergin would never get used to the god's speech. Each word said with perfect inflection, each syllable enunciated with the proper pronunciation, volume, intonation—flawlessly eloquent. A simple greeting uttered by anyone else would be powerless, the opening volley of meaningless small talk, but under the god's use—danger lay. It was the allure of the word that was his glamour. All gods had one, a means of seduction to make those of weak minds susceptible to influence. Amergin was no weak-minded fool, but the pull was great even for him—a skilled interlocutor who had apprenticed under Oghma's tutelage. *Greetings to you*—the salutation is the first of many stressors. It is the proclamation of opening engagement; Oghma noticed him. Then the question, *how do you fare?* So innocent a query, but from a god, he'd have to watch. He mustn't reveal too much else he'd end up bound by word.

"I am troubled."

"These are trying times that have come upon us. There are many pieces in motion now."

"Aye," Amergin sighed, "but 'afore I return ta my charge, is all in readiness with the Covenant? I will need ta apprise the priestess prior ta the start o' the ceremony."

"Yes. There is a list of proposals from the Tuatha Dé and the Formorians. You will have the other?"

"Aye. We will be prepared. My concern is for the other matter."

He looked off in the distance, "There is unrest. A thirteenth has not yet been chosen to replace the one they lost. It will be one from their ranks, an unseasoned initiate. It draws close to the eve of his appointment."

"They think ta compel her…"

Oghma pursed his lips and paced away. Amergin waited, knowing that omniscience wasn't in the god's aptitude.

"Come, we will consult the Well of Segais. There we might ascertain the path in which to follow."

In all his years he had never visited the well. Travel with a god was efficient in the moral realm, vast distances covered in mere minutes. Travel in Tir-Na-Nog was instantaneous.

Before any thought coalesced in his mind, he was pushing aside branches to reveal a lovely secluded spot, dappled in shadow. A lovely, but unassuming environ guarded by the forest hid its secrets. Here past, present, and future melded together. It was a place where knowledge superseded time. Soon he'd have access to all things known in the past. He'd be able to see the truth in the present. He'd be able to use both to accurately navigate the future. A selfish desire housed in all men's hearts surged, and Amergin knew why after millennia of watching men kill for it, the quest to find it, control it, and weld its power; the gods contrived for it to slip into human myth. The urge to use it selfishly was too great a temptation; and now the God of Communication invited him to its banks.

Amergin closed his eyes and inhaled through his nose until his lungs couldn't take any more. He held his breath, focusing on his heartbeat. He exhaled before he had the need to breathe again, only to repeat the process.

"We will begin when you are ready."

He opened his eyes to find Oghma squatting on the opposite bank trailing his fingers in the water.

"Proceed without me. I cannae guarantee…"

The god considered him for a moment, "Can I ask what the need is that makes this so desirable?"

Amergin sat where he was on the grass knowing that since the god was reposed he ought to be as well lest he offend. "Why do ye want ta know?"

"My dominion leaves me…curious. Knowledge fuels communication and therefore should improve relations, but from what I observed it only brings conflict ad infinium."

"When I was young, truly, as gauged by human years, e'en 'afore I was selected ta be Reliquary, I was strong o' mind and body." He snorted at a flash of a memory brought to mind a humiliating turn of events involving a woman. "Well, maybe it was just strength o' body. Anyway, what I speak o' is a' one time my back was straight, my legs, arms, and chest were knotted with muscle."

"Of course," the god nodded, "but this was before you harnessed the Auld Ways."

"Aye, but I speak o' another type o' strength. I bested men twice my size for the briefest o' moments, and then it was gone." He looked down at his hands, spotted and worn. "I used ta be able ta split wood for the fire with one fell o' my ax. Now, I cannae hold it above my head and bring it down with any force without my arms trembling."

"That is your mortal coil."

"T'is a burden we must bear, but knowledge is its own power, one no' dependent on strength o' muscle. It doesnae atrophy with time."

"When you became the Reliquary, and even more so when you passed that mantle for the Myrddin, you are among the strongest…"

"Magic, aye." Static sparked between Amergin's outstretched hands growing in intensity between his fingers; his hands molded it as one would a handful of snow, electricity sparking blue within its molded sphere. He clapped his hands squelching the energy, the sparse soft hairs on the backs of his hands erect from proximity. "But e'en now there are those who surpass me—I doonae covet her abilities nor his, mind ye; but ha' only a quick regret that my time is coming ta a close. I willnae be here ta see the renewal o' the Covenant." He chortled, "My greatest achievement by far was besting the gods—no offense."

"Tread carefully, mortal."

He bowed his head, "Aye, forgive me, I speak out o' turn."

The god stroked his beard, a peculiar idiosyncrasy indicating reflection. They were usually so staid that for one of them to fidget like a human and show vulnerability was frightening. Not often was a mortal present for divine contemplation, and Amergin was the last to want that to become a common occurrence. He needed the boundaries to be clear.

"I begin to understand. Without knowledge you

would not have been able to deceive us."

"Without knowledge *and* understanding, I wouldnae ha' been able ta pull off the ruse. All the assembled miscalculated the new contenders."

"Most were…still are, feeble and dull-witted."

"And ye've paid for yer arrogance. So concerned ye were with the formidable strength o' the Formorians that ye underestimated the danger on the other front."

There was a movement in Oghma's eyes, a shifting of color. Inky blackness filled the space and radiated outward over his cheeks.

Amergin backpedaled and cowered before the god, "I beg yer pardon, my lord." He quaked, prostrate before him, "F…f… forgive."

The god surged forward so he towered over the Myrddin. He stood still for a long moment and then the color receded from his cheeks and his eyes became clear again. He offered his hand to Amergin who took it. The god repositioned his grip and pulled the man to his feet. "It was a lesson never to be repeated."

"Then take action now. The Coven intends ta supplant the priestess, taking her abilities and shift power in their favor. What will they be able ta dae once that happens? Summon the Reliquary, and gi' both o' us leave ta protect yer asset."

"He is the charge of Cernunnos."

"All the better. Cernunnos has an added stake in this. She is his daughter. He'll want her safe."

Oghma strode to the water's edge and squat down. Amergin watched as Oghma pull out chunks of water reeds and throw them over his shoulder by the bank of the Well and dig in the mud until he had a small area cleared with water just on the surface. He was amused by the similarities the deity had to a child playing in the mud for the first time. The only, unsettling difference was that the child would have been covered from elbow to ear in muck, but the god was pristine. No mud caked on his velvet brocade sleeves, neither his hands, nor fingernails shown any dirt, even though Amergin saw him dig.

Oghma bent to write in the mud with his index finger. His hand glowed in the creases of his knuckles and the nailbeds, and as he formed the letters the same lumination spread to the script. The water rushed in to cover each letter as soon as he finished but a trace of luminescence was left for a moment until the next was started. Amergin couldn't see what he wrote, but how many had the priviledge to see the God of Communication, the one responsible for the creation and teaching of the Druid alphabet, compose. There was no comparison. He made the most painstakingly, beautiful illuminated text look like chicken scratch and he was playing in the mud.

His pace quickened and the sleeves of his robe were a hindrance. He tore at the frog closures and let the garment fall off his shoulders. The minute it settled on the grass, Amergin could see darkness creep up from the hem trailing in the water, and the mud splatters half way up the sleeves. A thought sparked in his mind that this was somehow important. The robe was not enchanted itself but only when it was on the god. He put it to the back of his mind and again gave his attention to the god.

Divested of the brocade and velvet robe, Oghma was clothed in a white alb and a brown homespun chasuble much like the garments worn by the Roman clerics. He had never seen such simple clothes on a god, and he wondered if the simplicity was significant in some way to his dominion in contrast to his outer robe. He must ask if he had the opportunity in the future.

Oghma was by this time writing with both hands in deference to the rate in which he now wrote. The shallow pool was aglow. He finished with a flare and scooped a large section out with his two hands. He molded it and chanted, *"Lig é a bheith ar eolas."* Let it be known, Amergin mindlessly translated. The viscosity of the mud changed into the consistency of clay. Oghma blew on the packed ball igniting the same glow and he squeezed the ball. The clay crumpled and fell from his hands leaving a glowing spherical lattice. He blew on it again, and it dispersed like the seeds of a dandelion. Carried on remnants of his breath, they swirled low over the water, until the wind caught them and carried them away.

~ ~ ~

They didn't have to wait long before Cernunnos and Alex arrived. While the gods conferred, Alex greeted Amergin with a hearty pat on the back. "How goes it, old man?"

Amergin shrugged his shoulders, "Wish we met again under better circumstances, but t'is for the gods ta decide when ta make the next move."

"What's happened?"

"How much dae ye ken?"

"When I left Brenawyn in the mortal realm I was compelled by Cernunnos, but he promised ta stay the Hunt 'til she came ta him 'afore Samhain. Finvarra came ta me soon afterward and told me that she underwent Widdershins and she made her way ta William."

"Nothing else? Are ye sure?"

Alex nodded, intentionally keeping quiet about his knowledge of the pregnancy.

"Och." He looked to the gods, and grabbed Alex, "Ye need ta come back with me. There's much that has happened."

Alex grabbed a handful of Amergin's cloak, "She's no' safe? Tell me."

"She caused a clishmaclaver when she arrived that's for sure. Arrived first thing and there were those that called her the Sleeping Lady."

Alex groaned slapping his hand to his forehead.

"That could ha' been easy o'erlooked but then

there was the child."

Panicked, Alex asked, "What child?" a decibel or two higher than he intended. His voice carried and the gods looked at them.

Amergin yanked Alex so his back was to the deities. "Keep yer voice down, man."

He closed his eyes and inhaled through his teeth, "What child?" he asked again in an impatient whisper.

"One o' yer brother's groomsmen's babes. Sickly from birth as William tells it."

"What o' it then?"

"She healed her in Hall, 'afore everyone and the gods. There was nay way ta hide who she was after that."

Horror struck Alex as the scenarios played out in his head. She was in the past, a stranger, no family to protect her, and those that would help could only do so much, her speech different, her mannerisms; she was independent and that alone might brand her a witch.

"Did ye no' tell her that ta declare herself was tantamount ta heresy now?"

"Argh, I didnae get a chance ta. Her time is so verra much different and I only had a short time."

"William called me ta steal her away 'afore the bishop came. He was afraid that he'd bring the witch hunters. There were rumors—Relax. We got away."

"Ah, she was with ye. There's no one I would trust more—

"There is one other thing, Alex."

"Aye?"

Amergin backed up and planted his feet, "Liam."

Anger boiled over, "That whoreson! I'll kill him." He stalked to Amergin intent on violence. He shook his balled fists, "And ye left her exposed ta come here? Are ye daft then?"

"I left her under guard, two score o' men, William wouldnae ha' it any other way. They're under Tavish's command."

"Tavish, ye say? He's a braw fighter, but why, Amergin? Ye ken her importance. Why would ye leave when ye are the best equipped ta defend?"

"Oghma got word ta me that the Coven were preparing, so under guise, I traversed time, infiltrated their compound ta ascertain the threat."

"Were ye recognized?"

Amergin gave him a withering look. His bones creaked and he tilted his head to the sky. Alex could see his facial bones moving under skin. "Ye seem ta forget, fledgling, that I am the master of disguise." Amergin brought his head down to look Alex in the eye.

Alex was looking into the eyes of his brother, and had the disguise been complete with height and girth his own mother would have mistaken him for her son.

"Ye also seem ta forget that I got Pendragon's father past the guard ta his mother's bedchamber."

"That was a long time ago, old man, when are ye

going ta let it go? An ill-begotten tryst, that ended with Arthur fated ta lead such a sad life. I'd no' be so smug about yer dealings in that game. I know where he is, and I'm no' sure that he'd consider it a blessing."

"Och, a'right then."

"And the threat?"

"Cormac is getting ready ta move. He has no' appointed a twelfth ta take the Oracle's place yet. He means ta do so on Samhain 'afore he tries ta take the priestess' powers."

"Any intelligence on how he…"

"He has a hostage. A healer was summoned ta tend ta her so she can undergo travel."

"It can be one of two women. How old?"

"A young lass, hair shorn close ta the scalp, a shame really. She was quite bonny."

"Shite. T'is Maggie."

Chapter 20

Maggie flailed, pummeling blindly as she awoke to a gag being shoved in her mouth. Large hands caught her wrists before she brought them down again and pinned the one closest to her assailant to the cement. A knee slammed into her bicep grinding it further. She bucked, trying to dislodge him, kicking out with her legs. A work lamp was switched on. She saw the filament flicker before the full wattage distorted her vision. She turned her head away from the painful light seeing spots dance in her field of sight. The man attempted again, but she clamped her jaw shut as she tried to press her face into the wall. Her movement was hindered by the pinned arm, his knee ground into the muscle pinching as she shifted. Tears tracked across the bridge of her nose, a wincing pain, and then she was free. She windmilled the arm to bring it close to her body and pressed it close to her side as she hid her face at the base of the wall.

Her assailant grabbed a fistful of her shorn hair and yanked. The short hair slipped out of his fingers and she bashed her nose against the wall, making her eyes tear more. He reached around and grabbed her nose, pinching the nostrils, and pulled her face toward him. His other hand clamped around her throat. She clawed at his wrist. He grunted, and locked his elbow pressing down until she reflexively opened her mouth in a futile attempt to gulp at the air. He stuffed the wadded fabric in her mouth making her gag, but she could breathe. She inhaled through her nose, and she smelled blood; her own or his, it didn't matter.

She was yanked up and spun around; her hands secured behind her back. The coarse rope bit into her wrists and she strained to keep the muscles tight as he wound the rope around, binding her. The same hood, from the smell of it, materialized as it was being put over her head. She was being moved again.

What had the healer said? *Be compliant. Go with them without a fight—not fucking likely.*

She could see little through the fabric of the drawstring hood, but she could tell when the punishing light from the 500 watt work lamp was shut off. She let out a sigh of relief as if the light held in it its own form of punishment. It also meant she was quite literally in the dark again.

She felt her assailant move away from her, but now there were more bodies in the space. Their determined steps echoed off the walls.

"Please," she sobbed, "Please, don't do this."

She took a step back feeling for the wall behind her with her fingertips. She lurched backward, stumbling over the discarded blanket, and her shoulder blades made contact. She slid along the wall until she reached the corner. There, bolstered on both sides, she cowered knowing nothing she did would help her now.

The overhead fluorescent light was on, she could see from the slivered space the open drawstring left when she moved just right. There were hands on her shoulders again, smaller but just as intent. The owner towered over her. She bent her hand and sniffed. Antiseptic soap and cigarettes, the smell of a new pack just opened. *Andy.*

She leaned against him putting her head on his chest. His reaction was small, but in the confined space, she felt him shudder. He put an arm around her waist rubbing the small of her back ever so briefly. Something, a broomstick perhaps, fell and clattered against the shelving, and the moment was gone. He grabbed her and led her out of the maintenance closet. Maggie banged into the doorjamb; Andy muttered an apology.

A cold draft prickled her skin beyond the threshold, but she was cocooned in a scratchy wool wrap instantly as if the person was waiting for her to emerge. Andy bent suddenly, scooping her up in a fireman's hold, one arm behind her knees securing her to his chest and the other on her hip guiding her to a comfortable spot as he rolled his shoulder to evenly distribute her weight.

It wasn't at all comfortable. The hold was meant for those too incapacitated to feel the bony shoulder digging into the abdomen. Upside down, the ends of her wrap flopped down to cover her head, but no one had seen to secure the drawstring of the hood. It hung on the edge of her chin, and she thought with any luck no one would notice when it slipped off from Andy's movement, and her bumping into his back.

He patted her rump familiarly.

She tensed at the audacity of the borderline violation. She was confined inside the coil of fabric with her arms crossed over her chest. If she resisted she'd only manage to look like an inchworm. She hoped it was a long way to wherever they were destined, and she further hoped that her weight crippled him.

Blood pooled in her head and after a short time she imagined could feel her blood pressure pulse in her temples. She had good balance, but this angle, and being confined so, was disorienting.

That was his plan all along.

He even told her as much when he brought her up the stairs in the wheelchair. He aimed to keep her disoriented: first she was sedated, then made dependent on him for her sustenance, her bodily eliminations…and hygiene. She was kept in the dark, forced to wear a hood, and moved only at night. He used the work lamp to further disorient her, and now the wool prison. Resting her head against his back made her neck absorb the shock of his gait. It took strength to resist the jostling which further added to her neck pain. In contrast, allowing her head to thump against his back was a strain on her abdominal muscles and it made her head pound. She was nauseous and with repetition, she had to fight the urge to vomit swallowing bile as it filled her mouth.

She lost that battle and retched. Andy stopped when he felt the telltale muscle contractions.

"Why do ye stop? Time is o' the essence."

Andy put his arm around the back of her knees, and a hand on her back as he bent over.

"Unless you want her to choke on her own vomit, I suggest we pause. Little good she would serve if she were dead."

"Ruadan is impatient. A punishment is sure ta be meted out."

"Then tell him it was me who made the decision to delay. I will meet his reckoning."

Cormac paused. "What dae ye need?"

Andy ripped off the hood, and wiped the vomit from Maggie's face tossing it away. "Water, towels, and a sharp knife."

Cormac looked down at him assessing, then unsheathed the dirk at his waist. He handed it to him hilt first. "Doonae make me regret this."

Water and towels were brought. Andy doused the towel and washed Maggie's face. She was grateful even though she knew it was at Andy's word she was treated this way. She had seen abuse, and lived through it time and again; she had an imagination, too, to tell her it could be so much worse. It wasn't completely hopeless...yet.

He tilted a bottle of water to her mouth. She clamped onto the opening and tried to guzzle it. He wrenched it from her, scolding her that she'd get sick, but it was too late. She fell to her side to vomit again. Andy sat her up and repeated the process. This time he gave her instructions to just swish the water in her mouth to get rid of the taste. She listened.

"Can you remain standing for a few minutes?"

Maggie nodded and Andy set her on her feet. He undid the wrap, uncoiling it the six times it was wrapped around her body. He measured it out, and taking the knife Cormac had entrusted him with, he slit the fabric, cutting it down by half. He balled up one piece and threw it at Linda. It hit her in the chest and she let it fall. She scowled and flipped him off, as she walked away. With the other he whisked it over Maggie's head, the length settling on her shoulders.

He called for Cormac again, asking this time for fasteners. Cormac came back with kilt pins. Andy put one in his front pocket, and opened the other putting the end in his mouth. He reached down to the edge of the trailing fabric and brought it up to Maggie's shoulder. He fastened it with the first on the pins, and then repeated the action on the other side. The last thing he did was saw at the binding holding her hands.

"There, that should be better."

He handed the knife back to Cormac and turned to pull the excess fabric to the front. He scooped Maggie up to cradle her in his arms. "Arrange the cloth so you're not cold."

"I can walk."

"Not possible."

"Why have the healer fix my leg then?"

He looked at her for a moment without answering, and then steeled his face. He pivoted to where Cormac stood behind him. "Let us not keep this Ruadan waiting."

~ ~ ~

The localized flushed fever receded with her headache and nausea making Maggie feel much revived. She had her head on Andy's chest to give the appearance she was still disoriented, but she was keenly aware. There were warehouses all around, but she couldn't grasp where they were. To her knowledge there was no place that was so big that would support the length of time a fairly large party had been walking with one member carrying a human-sized bundle without drawing attention. And when they had used the van to transport her in the past, why would they walk now?

They entered the last warehouse on the pier. It was empty, a vacuous space four stories high. There was an office immediately on the left. Actually, more of a guard house, with an automated wooden gate barring entrance to trucks entering from the hanger door.

Cormac walked to the center, his voice boomed out, "Ruadan." His baritone echoed eerily. "We are here as ye requested."

"As I can see," a deep voice answered.

"Show yerself, and ha' done with it. We followed yer rules."

"I shall be the judge. T'is my neck that will be on the chopping block if ought goes wrong."

"Yer more eager than I ta be done with the Covenant—

"Aye, t'is the truth, what ye speak, but if all is no' in readiness we willnae be able ta break the bounds o' the agreement that hold me in such…ugh…impotent form."

"Come then, approach, and see that we ha' complied."

There was a thud in the shadowed recesses of the warehouse, followed by the appearance of a man walking toward the group.

Andy put Maggie on her feet and took off his belt. He held out her hands instructing her to hold them there and cinched his belt around her waist. He fussed with the folds of the fabric, making sure the wool covered the linen dress underneath. Maggie look at him, and for the first time, saw fear in his eyes.

Cormac was the first to greet the man, placing both hands over his heart he bowed low. "Greeting to ye, my lord."

The man walked past without slowing to stand in front of Maggie. He was massive, making Andy and even Cormac look tiny…and bare-chested. Thick, corded muscle lay thick on his chest, springy dark hair trailed to the waist band of his leather pants accentuating the muscle tone of his abdominals. His arms were amply muscled too; his biceps appeared thicker than Maggie's waist. His hair was long and dark, and a full beard emphasized his strong jaw.

He stood there waiting for something, but Maggie was unsure what. She looked at Andy, only then made aware that her mouth was hanging open.

"Kneel in front o' yer god, girl."

Her head whipped back to the man, and a giggle escaped her lips. "My…god?"

Andy moved behind her and forced her down bending her head toward her chest. She could feel his hands tremble as he gripped her shoulders.

She caught his meaning. *God he wasn't, but that didn't mean she wasn't in acute danger, so if this man wanted her to kneel, by all that was sacred, she'd assume the position.*

"This slip o' a wench will be compulsion enough?"

"Aye." Cormac lied, and for the first time doubt crept in. He didn't know for sure, but it was a calculated risk. There were only two weaknesses that the priestess had; this girl was one of them.

"Yer willing ta risk yer life…yer soul on this

decision? If I open the passage, t'is an open declaration o' revolution."

"What choice dae we ha' now? We ha' come too far ta go back. I cannae traverse the realms o' time and place with so many that canna travel by Widdershins. There has ta be a modicum o' ability and she has none. The catalyst ta their undoing and she's stuck in this mortal realm. We are prepared. We must declare."

"So be it then." Ruadan ripped open a passage. Maggie had seen just the same done in the forest glen the afternoon she was taken only from a distance. Now, she saw what lay beyond. Colorful, undulating movement and sound lured her closer, and before she had a moment to think, Andy's hands were on her shoulders piloting her through the opening.

Chapter 21

Alex squatted by the waterside and trailed his fingers through the mirrored surface. The ripples radiated outward setting the tall waterweeds to sway on the other side. Regret filled Alex's heart. *As Reliquary he knew everything; as a man, he understood nothing. He was too callous after centuries of overzealous searching, jumping at the slightest provocation. All the women who came before, on second inspection, had nothing but overt displays of meager talent. He knew that the Lughnasadh ritual was not strong enough to bring Brenawyn's latent abilities, however strong, to the surface because he didn't fully understand the significance the night before. Asking permission, gods, how could he have been that stupid?*

It had been so long since he felt the touch of a woman. She knew him not for who he was, but just as a man. It had been too long since anyone had looked at him like that. He romanced her with stories of old and her innocent touch set his loins on fire. He wanted nothing but to forget in her arms for a while.

Selfish.

Thinking back to the ritual, the minute she had stepped into the circle he felt the magic sizzle to life.

He was surrounded by the blissfully ignorant thinking the ritual nothing but theater, but her grandmother knew the truth.

In his mind's eye, too late to spare her, he traced the patterns down her body remembering where each color gave into the next. In her palm a rounded spiral with three arms turning toward the center, the triskele, glowed scarlet. From there what appeared to be a single green band looped and knotted around itself as it alternately passed under and over at points stopping to create a blue spiral or gold triquetra.

Ripples. He splashed at the surface to obliterate his reflection. Here was where her fate was sealed. Nimue herself had seen to it, manipulated the events to make it seem as if it was Brenawyn's choice; but it never was. Nimue pressed her into servitude, made it necessary for her to leave her family behind; but he was the one who started her on the path. He brought her here. He shouldered the blame and the responsibility.

Alex was a sheep following his gods, being led by those same shepherds in the direction they chose: left at the crofter's cottage, across the glen, right to travel along the fence, and then off the cliff to his eternal damnation.

He had damned her to the same fate; but he would do it all over again. He was weak. He wanted her. He needed her. He loved her…and that he couldn't forgive himself for.

Alex surged to his feet and stalked to Cernunnos demanding, "Gi' me yer leave ta retur…" he paused. Deciding, he drew himself up to his full height and stepped closer to the god, fists clenched at his side. "Fuck! I am going whether ye wish it or no'."

Before Cernunnos could answer, he pivoted and strode away ripping open a passage to the mortal realm. He stepped through, not bothering to close it behind him.

~ ~ ~

His bones were lengthening and changing shape as he stepped through the veil. He paused just outside for the the familiar and painful breaking of his legs to form the structure of the wolf's hock completing the hind legs. He stifled his scream. It was agonizing pain for a brief moment, and then it lessened, became bearable with the accelerated knitting of new bone. He dropped to all fours, and shook, aiding the emergence of his pelt.

He squirmed out of his clothes, and turned to dig a hole in the soft loam. He dragged his clothes in, covering them with dirt, tramping on it the best he could in this form, and urinated on the spot. He couldn't take his clothes with him, and to have them found would draw unneeded suspicion. Wolf urine would keep the most inquisitive animals away as they smelled a predator, and in his experience what animals shied away from, humans generally did the same.

Alex and the Wolf both recognized the rolling hills by his brother's Keep. It wasn't in sight and that was just as well. He dismissed a pang of homesickness, he'd have liked to see Willie again, but he wasn't coming home. He wished he had questioned Amergin more to ascertain where along the route the company was. The Wolf's senses would have to do to pick up their scent. Two dozen horses and riders wouldn't be hard to find in an area that seldom saw a traveling pair.

He turned, hearing a wheezing breath behind him to find Amergin picking his way through the opening.

"Ye ha' a set o' stones on ye, boy!" He let out a guffaw that bent him over, hands on his knees, wheezing to catch his breath. "Ye should ha' seen his face. He didnae conceive ye would e'er be so brazen. Ye took him by surprise. Ye'll ha' ta deal with that sooner or later." He looked at the Wolf over his shoulder, and sighed. "Later…ye can deal with that later."

He straightened, putting most of his weight on the walking stick, stretching his back. "*Ooof,* I am getting too old for this." He closed the passageway. "Neednae ha' anything else ta worry about slipping through." He rubbed his hands together then unbuttoned his cloak and folded it over his arm. He snickered, looking toward the disturbed ground. "Ne'er did figure out what ta dae with yer trews? Good, ye deserve it. Dae ye ken that Mistress Fordoun still yammers on about yer penchant for losing yer clothes?"

Alex heard, but Amergin didn't need him to reply, so he sat and sighed, which came out as a very dog-like whine. When Amergin got underway it was across the glen, not the road as Alex had thought. They reached the tree line and Amergin balled up his cloak and pressed it into the base of the nearest oak. He divested himself of the rest of his garments until he stood naked as a babe. Gooseflesh covered his crepe skin. His back was to Alex, who could see the toll the centuries had exacted from this man. The crooked posture, the hunched back, made his knobbed spine more pronounced. He could count the vertebrae and ribs. His spindly legs shook from the mild exertion. Alex's canine senses identified him as sickly, weak…vulnerable to attack.

"Come, travel will be verra much quicker if we take the way of the hawk."

Alex was glad Amergin didn't turn around to face him because he imagined he'd see more of the ravages of time. He was also glad that he had shifted prior to Amergin's arrival. He wasn't sure if he'd be able to keep his pity in check. He shifted and felt his bones hollow and feathers sprout. He took to wing beside his mentor, screeching into the morning's sky, in part to mourn the years this man had lost.

They found the party not long after. Circling in the air, Alex was confused. Now back in the mortal realm he felt the imminent approach of the fire feast as if the very earth paused before exhaling. As one of her creatures he was more attuned; she was waiting, anticipating…he could almost hear her heartbeat. The party should have been rounding out their journey, but they were days out still.

Something was wrong.

He descended to perch on a tree branch on the outskirts of their camp still under the guise of the hawk. Amergin landed further back. The camp was eerily quiet. The requisite men guarded it and those around the campfire were armed, swords drawn and lying within reach. There was no sign of Brenawyn.

Amergin, fully clothed in the same garments he had left folded under the oak, walked underneath the tree in which Alex was perched. He looked up and signaled for him to stay put.

From his vantage point he had a wide view of the entire site. Amergin walked up, making more noise than necessary. It was purposeful on his part, not wanting to cause alarm. The men would know long before he crossed the outskirts that someone was approaching in the open. The men in question began to move subtly. By the fire one got to his feet to put another log on to burn, and returned to his previous seat closer to his weapons, the guards posted on the outskirts moved in concert to intercept the newcomer.

Amergin whistled, stopping them in their tracks, and their movement changed. It was a collective sigh and camp life resumed its normal course. The guards met Amergin and after a brief exchange, Alex was motioned to approach. Having no clothes in which to change, he had no choice but to remain as the Hawk.

Amergin met him.

"We are to rendezvous with Tavish. He's tracking Liam. His wife and the priestess…"

There was no time to change, rage surfaced, and Alex took to flight, circling low around Amergin. He dove at his head catching the man's forearm as he brought it up. His talons dug in, but Amergin was quick. Motioning for the guards to stand down, he turned, unclipping his cloak and spiraled it out to cover Alex's hawk form. His interlace flared to life, and dismissing his arm that had been ripped to the bone from the deadly talons, he held tight, ending up on his knees bent over the bird pinning him to the ground. He stayed this way for a long time, even after Alex stopped fighting.

"Ye waste yer energy and precious time by fighting me." Amergin said, as he felt the tension leave Alex. "I'm going ta let go my hold. Are ye composed enough?"

He waited another moment and then released the hawk, sitting back on his heels. He let Alex squirm his way out of the cloak's folds. Alex shifted back into human form, pulling the discarded cloak onto his lap to cover his nakedness. Amergin gave a nod, and returned to tend his arm, already glowing with the working of a healing spell.

"I am sairy."

"Doonae apologize. I understand."

"I could ha' hurt ye. I wanted ta kill ye.

"Ye didnae want ta."

Alex scoffed, motioning to the damaged arm, "Och, ye nay think so?"

"Nay, I doonae."

"Just one more thing I'm sairy for," he muttered more to himself than for Amergin's ears.

"Let it bide, Alexander. I wouldnae ha' let ye if ye did mean it."

"Oh?"

"Aye, ye arrogant bastart! I may be old and feeble, gods ken my body is failing me, but as long as magic runs in my blood, ye'd ha' a time trying ta best me."

From the flush in his cheeks, and the look of shame on his face it was apparent to Alex that the encounter affected him more than he let on.

Amergin got to his feet and stumbled, reaching out to catch himself on the trunk of the nearest tree. He walked off without giving Alex a second look. "Let us go find Tavish and the priestess."

~ ~ ~

Maggie was conducted through the opening, her heart hammering in her chest. She knew that she was leaving the world she knew behind. A world that didn't make a bit of sense, and one she regularly thought she didn't have a place in, but things were logical. It followed the laws of physics—gravity, that was a good solid example. Gravity made sense. Ripping a whole in thin air like it was fabric did not. Furthermore, stepping through that tear to another dimension definitely did not! *But, magic was real.* This statement echoed in her mind, and she forced it out.

Andy stepped through after her, his hands firmed planted on her shouldered directing her further in. All around them were trees, more vibrant, as if the color spectrum exploded and expanded indefinitely. And the trees were individual yet part of the surrounding forest, so lush and packed with growth, much like the pictures of the rainforest she'd seen in National Geographic; but this was a forest, she could identify some of the specimens. She didn't know where or when she learned to distinguish one from the other, having no personal experience in either, but she knew she was *elsewhere*.

Magic is real. The thought surfaced again.

The passage was closed behind her; she heard the vacuum close with a pop. Until then, she hadn't registered the cacophony until it stopped. Silence settled over them like a heavy blanket, she could feel the pressure on her eardrums. The colors intensified and the undulation started again in earnest. She'd seen it before when she was standing at the threshold to this world thinking then that it was fibers in the air, motes of dust, pollen, petals from flowering trees… but here she saw that it was more. Everything was moving.

Andy's hands left her shoulders and she glanced back; he had the same wonderment on his face. She moved closer to a fern at the edge of the path. She reached out to touch a frond and it recoiled, pulling each of the blades toward the rachis. She snatched her hand back. The reaction sparked a wave of motion, each frond withdrawing like the first. Even the fiddleheads at the soil's surface curled inward toward the ground. She looked to Andy for an explanation, but his eyes were as big as saucers.

She moved to the middle of the path bumping into Andy as she retreated. The ferns though, began to move in reverse motion, opening back up one after another, the wave motion like a domino effect. They undulated again and burst outward, each dancing color a separate entity around Maggie and Andy. Flitting here and there, landing on her skin, her eyelashes, up her nose. She batted at it, sneezing. The motes drew back all at once from the disturbance, but flew in again more insistent, tunneling through her short hair. Feather-soft wings brushed her neck. A small dragonfly she thought at first, but then she thought she saw...one landed on the back of her hand as she was bringing it up to her face and there it was... a small faery? It was smaller than her pinky nail, so small she couldn't even discern whether it was male or female, if they even had the distinction. It was humanoid: two arms and legs, facial features two large eyes, a nose, a mouth. And wings made of what looked like an iridescent membrane, twice as large as its own body.

A large hand swatted at them from behind and she swung around to Cormac. He scowled, "Forest dryads. They are curious. T'is no' often mortals enter without an inkling o' magic."

She nodded as if that made any sense to her.

"Come, we must no' delay."

Andy took her hand.

"You're not going to carry me?" she asked sardonically.

"No need to any longer. There's nowhere for you to go. You can't get back the way you came, and to chance it on your own here? There are things that lurk here that are worse than your nightmares. Best to stay with the evil you know."

Ruadan opened another passage, holding back this time until everyone was through. He took a particular interest in Maggie. She could feel his eyes bore into her back as she passed. The hairs at her nape stood on end, and she gulped, trying hard not to turn back and look. She had a feeling she'd find him too close. When he stepped through, his shadow devoured hers.

"Mortal girl," his voice boomed out, "yer fear makes ye all the more enticing. Ye'll scream for me before I'm through."

Maggie cringed. Andy put his arm around her pulling her close.

Ruadan's laugh made the ground shake. "Brave for one who's so weak. I will kill ye quickly when the time comes."

Maggie quickened her step, "The evil I know, huh? Holy fuck!" and all Andy could do was nod.

Cormac pointed, "Come, we've lodgings for the night."

They came through to a different place. There were no warehouses, or busy streets. No cars, buses, or people for that matter. There was a narrow road leading to a group of buildings she could see in the distance. The buildings were small little specs almost indistinguishable except for their linear construction and formation. The road was not paved but well-worn, with two deep furrows approximately five feet apart. Wagons? Can't be. Where were the cars? Weird.

She could feel the sweat drip between her shoulder blades despite the nip in the air. Her bare feet were the only part of her that was cold, and they were cut up because no one had supplied her with shoes. She stepped on a sharp stone and cried out, hopping on one foot until she plopped on her backside in the midst of the road cradling her injured foot. She extracted the sliver of stone, thinking it was a shard of glass, and Andy went to scoop her up but was stopped by Cormac with a word.

"Doonae. T'is part o' her penance. She must endure."

Andy hesitated but thought better of it and walked on.

When they finally entered the village, Maggie was dragging she was in so much discomfort she missed the signs. She picked up her head and took in the thatched rooves and the stables filled with horses. She spun taking in much of the same scenery all around.

"Where…When are we?"

Cormac pivoted and dropped into a formal bow, "My lady, welcome ta 1457."

Chapter 22

Spencer snored and farted in his sleep somewhere nearby. Brenawyn nestled down further under the down comforter making sure to cover her nose and settling back against the solid form behind her cocooning her in warmth. There was a sleepy inquisitive murmur and a rolling of hips belying any interest in returning to a comatose state. She moved to pillow her head with her arm... and leaves crinkled. She bolted awake, but punishing fingers pressed into her hip pulling her back for more of his grinding. She could feel the state of matters through the layers of skirts.

"If this was what you wanted, I would have been happy to oblige you sooner." Liam crooned.

She scrambled to get her legs under her, pulling on her bindings until her hands turned a mottled red. She scooted around the trunk of the tree desperate to put something between them.

"Get the fuck away from me! I swear, I will kill you."

"Now, now." He chastised, but he didn't move from his original position. He patted the ground next to him. "Come on back."

"Fuck you, you sack of shit," she screamed.

"Your loss, then." He groaned and stretched, making a lewd show of adjusting his length smirking at her all the while before jumping to his feet.

Brenawyn recognized that smile and she couldn't believe that she ever found it alluring. It made her feel dirty and ashamed.

He stalked off, kicking Isla in passing. She cried out and grabbed her shin. She scuttled back against the base of her tree, inhibited by her bounds, but he didn't spare her a look. He walked to the horses, untying the reins and tossing them over the nearest one's head. He grasped a handful of the mane and swung up. The horse protested and reared trying to toss him, but he kept his seat and viciously kicked the withers making the animal squeal. The others in the pack strained at their leads. Liam was insistent, and they were off like a shot, trampling through the undergrowth.

"Are you all right?"

Isla rubbed her leg, "Feels like the fecking man snapped my leg, but aye, I suppose I am. And ye? Ye were marrit ta that clod?"

"A long time ago."

"Good riddance. Mayhap fortune will shine down, he'll get the pox and his cock will fall off!"

Brenawyn strained her neck in the direction he disappeared. "Where do you think he went?"

"Well, we're near Llanfair as best as I can tell. I heard them yammering on last night. Seems ta be takin' us ta Bryn Celli Ddu." She laughed at that, "if they are, mind ye, they'll be getting a surprise."

"Oh? Why's that?"

"That's were we were headed a' the first. My Tavish has kent long 'afore now that we're gone. He'll be followin' and god help the man who stands in his way."

"Why would they go through the effort to kidnap us if they knew we were headed to the same place? Why not ambush us later?"

"Perhaps they didnae intend ta do it," and shrugged her shoulders, "mayhap we just presented too good a target ta pass up. I'm that sairy for it. I should ha' thought...if anything happens ta ye...I'll ne'er forgive myself."

"What is in Bryn Celli Ddu?" Brenawyn stumbled on the name, feeling like her tongue had inexplicably grown to fill her mouth.

"T'is the Mound in the Dark Grove."

Brenawyn shook her head indicating that the explanation had no meaning for her.

"Nay? Hmm." She tilted her head considering Brenawyn. Apparently coming to the conclusion that she was just momentarily flummoxed, and deigning to be the epitome of unending patience she explained, "T'is the site o' the Covenant drawn, when Amergin duped the Tuatha Dé and the Formorians both."

Brenawyn thought back. What did she remember from Finvarra's history lesson? It was after the third battle of Magh Tuireadh, "'I am the shield for every head. I am the tomb for every hope?[1]' He told the gods to wait off shore and then used the time to weave a spell repelling them when they thought to advance if I remember correctly."

"Aye. T'is what sent them ta the land o' the sidhe, Tir-Na-Nog."

"Tell me more about this place, the Mound in the Dark Grove."

"Och, a henge and burial mound on the isle o' Anglesey. T'is said that there are two passageways that meet in the mid, one from this world, and one from Tir-Na-Nog. I was taught the stories ta pass on ta my bairns when the time came. We were ta stand clear o' it and the like; else we may be taken by the faerie. I always had a fair curiosity about it considering.

I suppose t'is good chance that t'is set for there. Out o' the prying eyes o' men. A dangerous task ye ha'," she glanced around, lowering her voice so much that Brenawyn had to strain to hear. "They'll brand ye a witch and anyone connected ta…"

She stopped, and bit her lip looking away.

"Didn't exactly sign up for dancing naked around the oak under the full moon, did you?"

Isla gave no answer.

Putting her head against the trunk of the tree, "Well, welcome to the club…" Brenawyn muttered,

---

[1] "Song of Amergin" translated by Robert Graves.

more to herself than Isla. "We have cookies."

They were on their way a little while later even though Liam hadn't reappeared. Maybe it was because of his absence, Brenawyn and Isla were allowed to ride unencumbered. Angry bleeding lesions circled her wrists and jute fibers stuck out porcupine-like from having her hands bound to trees at night and the pommel during the day. It was good to be rid of them, but the abraided skin burned from contact with the air and occasional brushes with the edges of her clothing.

Isla was riding ahead, her horse's harness tied to the lead guard. The three Brenawyn had accompany her surrounded her at a distance. Only the jiggling of the harnesses kept time as they picked their way through the woods until one of her guards, a relatively young man, took to whistling. She recognized the melody as one she heard at the Sinclair Keep, and soon Isla's voice joined in timidly. Her voice grew stronger when she wasn't immediately rebuked.

The sun was high overhead when the lead horse doubled back, the guard fumbling with the knot tying the horses together. The guard handed the end of the rope over.

"We are close. Follow a' a distance."

~ ~ ~

With the eye of the hawk and the olfactory senses of the wolf, Alex and Amergin found Tavish's trail not too long after they embarked. He had six men with him, trackers all. Their collective footprint minimal, they might have gone unnoticed if not for the heightened senses.

They went without horses, easier to move silently amid the trees though there was a chance that their target would outdistance them. They were too near Bryn Celli Ddu and with the fire feast looming Alex thought it a bad decision. Liam might take a calculated risk to run the last stretch in the open, stealth be damned.

Amergin howled and Alex swooped down, shifting before his talons touched ground. Two wolves now advanced, crouching low. They topped a rise overlooking a gully, and in it a group of five horses gave wide berth to an open glen, opting to hug the far embankment. His heart leapt in his chest when the one rider turned her head and he caught a glimpse of Brenawyn's profile.

The other woman in the party turned to glance in their direction and started singing. Alex looked to Amergin, but his eyes were fixed on a spot to their left. Alex sniffed the air: five, six, seven men lay within feet of them, one with his focus on their position. Tavish.

Lyrics drifted up. "*Quadrupeds shine and wander. Birds nest on blossoming branches. I cry joy[2]…*"

Tavish looked in her direction; an apparent signal

---

[2] From Cambridge Songs

worked out previously between the two. She knew that they were there.

Liam wasn't among the group. He might have ridden on ahead to make sure all was in readiness. He could see the end of the woods from this vantage point, and beyond it laid Llanfair. He could smell the hearth smoke from here, distinctive as it mingled amongst the scents of the copse, rutting stags and the scat of various wildlife, human sweat and dried urine…and fear.

Alex was beginning to fear proximity might make any sort of rescue attempt dangerous. Any attack would be loud and so close to the village, likely to attract attention. Men would be collateral damage; regrettable, but sometimes a foregone conclusion. The thing that had him most concerned now was a tree stump in the center of the glen. On it was an abandoned plate mounded with food. Its presence was the answer to why the party avoided the area.

It was the night before Samhain, the night of the Dumb Supper. For all that it was a Christian country, the Scots were a superstitious lot and traditions died hard. As a boy he scoffed at the nonsense. The tradition called for setting an extra place at the head of the table, the only day of the year that his father would give up that honor. Supper would be served but the choicest pieces would be set at the empty seat. After the meal was served and consumed in complete silence, the matriarch, Mrs. Fordoun, after his step-mother's death, would bring the plate to the woods as an offering—a bribe to the faerie. If the plate were empty by morning she'd know that her family was safe for the next cycle. It always was, except for that last year…

Now, Alex knew the utter futility of its observance. The gods were fickle and no amount of sacrifice would appease their wrath.

The veil was too thin between realms as the passageways opened heralding the coming of winter. Deities would be free to wander. Time folded in on itself; past, present, and future were one. If any gods were in the vicinity, and it was a good bet to say all of the more powerful ones and those of older ancestral lines, the truly frightening ones, were awaiting the Ban-Druidh ceremony. They were the ones who were called by name to reaffirm man's adherence to the Auld Ways as dictated by the Covenant. And this was just the formalities of the night's agenda.

The real intrigue of the night would be the successful navigation of the power play to which Brenawyn was just an unwitting pawn. She represented an unknown quantity; she was shrouded in mystery. Seers and even Aerten and Caer Ibormeith, the goddesses of fate and prophecy, could not discern her role. Fate could not be thwarted even by the gods, but here was a mere mortal woman who seemed to do just that. The powers of the high priestess aside, that was her real allure.

No. He'd have to hold back and wait, as much as he'd like to go in now and tear out the throats of the men who guarded her. He knew that they weren't who he needed to best, though they'd be part of the casualties tonight; and he wouldn't lose a moment's sleep over it. Even Liam and Cormac were only middlemen. Bathing in their blood would give him personal satisfaction for amassed transgressions; but they were the key to unraveling the conspiracy to dissolve the agreement thus making the mortal realm the battlefield of the gods again.

Attacking now would attract unwanted attention from the village. Those that had no direct role in the war or comprehension as to what was at stake would come into contact with elemental colossi. There would be heavy casualties he suspected in the impending battle and in good conscience he couldn't abide by more useless slaughter.

Alex was failing as Brenawyn's protector.

~ ~ ~

Bryn Celli Ddu looked like the faerie mound in her mind her grandmother often told them of. Mounded hillocks covered with grass greener than the surrounds. She couldn't see beyond the threshold, the darkness housed within seemed to consume the very sunlight.

Boulders lined the path pulling her toward gaping maw of the Mound of the Dark Grove. The ground became more uneven the closer she got, but her pace quickened as if she was on autopilot. Her footfalls remained uniform even though her consummate guards were stumbling trying to keep up.

She entered and the temperature dropped. She could see her breath on the air, and gooseflesh prickled her skin. Despite how it looked from the outside, some light made it in to the passageway, and she could see charred human remains. She reached down to scoop up some ash, saying a quick prayer for these nameless souls. Who better to show her the way? She blew on the ash reciting *Taispeaín an solas dom*. The phrase whispered in her mind by Finvarra, the last aid he gave her before she traveled back in time. The ash stirred in her open palm, whirling, it alighted. The ash raced out ahead of her, pinpricks of light, as far as she could see down the seemingly endless passageway.

She heard the others enter behind her but she paid them no mind. She was here. She knew what she had to do, best to get it done. Find Maggie, and then see if she could send her home before keeping her promise to Cernunnos.

Her leg muscles ached before the passageway opened up and expanded. The ash light looked like the night sky against the ceiling of the chamber. In contrast to the rough-hewn walls of the tunnel, the chamber was fashioned out of bedrock. Carved and polished, it reflected the lights, revealing the intricate friezes depicting the evolution of conquest: Fir Bolg,

Formorians, Tuatha Dé Danann, and the Milesians.

Someone cleared a throat in the shadows in front of her.

Brenawyn nearly jumped out of her skin. "Whose there?"

A woman emerged, her posture and step straight and light, but when she approached, Brenawyn could see she was an old woman. The ash lights illuminated her face in bluish hues that made her look even older.

"Hello. I am…"

"Priestess, I ken who ye are. T'is ye who doonae ken my name. I am Caileach, Woman of Winter. I am ta assist ye in preparations for the Ban-Druidh. Come, ye must wash and adorn yerself proper."

She led Brenawyn to a side antechamber that was markedly warmer because of the hot spring bubbling up in the center. Steam rose and curled invitingly and Brenawyn thought how good it would feel to wash away the grime of travel.

The woman left as she sank into its depths, reveling in the heat. The sand under her feet was coarse, and she used it to scrub her skin in the absence of soap. The woman returned too soon, with a folded garment in her arms. "When ye feel yerself ready."

She emerged and the woman shook out the garment and Brenawyn's mouth dropped open. She had seen this robe before. She'd worn it filling in for her grandmother at the summer solstice ceremony in

Salem. She reached out to stroke the emerald green embroidery. How did it get here? Or the question really was how did it come to be in her grandmother's possession?

"T'is how it was meant ta be."

"What?"

"The answer ta yer question."

Brenawyn stared blankly at her.

"Come, the time has come."

Brenawyn followed her out and the woman led her to a pedestal carved into a niche in the wall. She indicated with her hand the other niches at locations equidistant in the chamber. She bowed and backed away.

Turning, Brenawyn looked at the new candle and knew what she had to do. It was the same set up as the Lughnasadh ritual. If she could remember the words:

"I acknowledge the North Spirit…who gives me true bearing, guiding and calling me to my true home both time and place." With each word uttered, she gained more confidence. "I call to the wind, who lives companionably with the North giving me life-sustaining air to breathe. I summon both to this circle." She touched the wick and it sparked to life. "Let the flame of the candle mark my prayer."

Brenawyn moved to the second plinth. "I acknowledge the South Spirit, who awakens me to the promise and surprise of a new love, new life" she touched her abdomen, "a new day. I call to the Earth, who provides a continual food source and is the very ground I walk on." She touched the wick and it sparked to life. "Let the flame stand as sentinel. I summon both to this circle. Come and reside with me, rejoicing in the coming winter."

She moved to the third. "I acknowledge the West Spirit, who gives me comforting warmth and encourages me to seek new adventures—to craft my own destiny, to accept the mantle of priestess. I call to the Water, who quenches my thirst and heals my wounds." She touched the wick and it sparked to life. "Let the flame stand as sentinel. I summon both to this circle. Come and rest, for the coming of winter is the cocoon that precedes rejuvenation."

She moved to the last pedestal. "I acknowledge the East Spirit, who gives me rest for my weary body allowing me to replenish my mind, to seek out mentors to show me the Ways. I call to the Fire, who warms my hearth allowing me sight in the dark, and who is the full cycle of birth, destruction, and rebirth." She touched the wick and it burst to life. "Let the flame stand as sentinel. I summon both to this circle. Come and reside with me, rejoicing in the cycle of life."

Brenawyn moved to the center, raising her arms and voice. "I acknowledge the gods and goddesses of Old: Cernunnos, Epona, Belanus, Taranis, Blodevweld, Danu, and the Triple Mother Goddess. I offer my spirit to you. Let me be an extension of your will and of your Ways. Come join me in celebrating Samhain."

Caileach came to her, taking her elbow and lead her to a cushion placed in the space between where she was and the wall, and instructing her to kneel with her head bowed.

She could hear approaching footsteps from the passageway beyond. Silent figures emerged and moved in formation to similar cushions at equidistant points around the room. Cernunnos, Finvarra, and Oghma filed in to take their places. They were Tuatha Dé: tall, lithe, smooth alabaster skin, even Oghma whose age was evident, without wrinkles and each so beautiful one would never tire from looking at them. Their hair was silky, straight, and coiffed. Their attire fit for the most formal occasion. Finvarra acknowledged her with a tilt of his head.

Three others followed, representatives of the Formorians. She didn't recognize any of this group only their physical attributes seen in Finvarra's telling of the history of conquest. They were bigger, not notably in height, but in girth and muscle mass. Their hair was loose over their shoulders with braids decorated with bones, beads, and feathers. They were layered under leather and pelts but were adorned with ceremonial jewelry, intricately worked diadems and cloak fasteners. They took their place in the circle.

The last to enter were the Fir Bolg. Their appearance was so startling, her reaction drew the attention of those near her. They entered the chamber and straightened to their full height, towering over the other faerie. The Formor were Sidhe, Brenawyn reminded herself. The Sidhe were faerie, but not all faerie were Sidhe. Nomenclature was paramount if she wished to avoid insult; she imagined it would be like throwing a spark on this powder keg of an assembly.

Grey skin covered the Fir Bolg's muscle mass. The two males were bald except for a thick patch in the back that was slicked back and tied with a leather cord. They were naked except for a loincloth. The female had the side of her head facing Brenawyn plucked and tattooed. Most startling about her appearance was a puckered scar running along where her left breast should have been. Her dress or lack thereof, exposed this for all to see.

The last group, the Milesians, Brenawyn represented as their descendent. She was tiny in comparison, and woefully frailer; but yet the age of man ushered in by Amergin's covenant spoke of the evolutionary importance of adaptability, intuition and cunning over brute strength.

There were others now who filed in behind filling the space. There was more movement from behind her. Glancing back she saw Liam enter with Cormac, with Maggie in tow. Brenawyn moved to rise but was held in place by Caileach's stare. She looked back at both men who stood sneering, Liam adding insult to injury by inflicting pain. Maggie yelped and tried to squirm away, but he twisted her arm all the more and bent to lick her cheek—all for the benefit of Brenawyn's rage.

She felt the magic in her rise to her growing anger, but focused on the next entrants. Amergin was the next to enter with Tavish and others she recognized from the original guard. Amergin moved to take the one remaining cushion at her left. The gods, both seated and standing, hissed their displeasure at his participation in this ceremony. The Formorians rose ready to either fight or leave but were mollified by those near to resume their place.

It was Caileach who finally called the gathering to order. "T'is been many years that we ha' been a full contingent. The circle will be complete when the priestess declares herself." Turning to her, "Stand and declare before all who ye are."

Brenawyn stood, her height dwarfed by the faerie gathered, and she stammered, intimidated by their massive bulk. "My na..na. name is…" she panicked searching for a friendly face, but Maggie was engulfed by the crowds. Amergin was stone-faced, and then she caught a glimpse of Liam. She'd not declare herself a McAllister. She cast everything related to him away and found her strength. "My name is Brenawyn Margaret Leoncha Callahan." Her words echoed in the cavernous chamber. "I am the high priestess come to restore balance." There was a collective sigh, and a nod from Caileach.

"Name yer proxy, priestess."

"My proxy? What do I need a…"

"I will serve as the priestess' proxy." A deep tenor behind her declared.

Brenawyn swung around, recognizing Alex's voice. Tears sprang to her eyes, so happy and relieved she was to see him. He motioned for her to remain where she was. His declaration caused a murmur, and cries rose, undistinguishable at first, then Cormac's deep baritone called out, "He cannae. He is already named as such by the Myrddin. He cannae be proxy ta both."

"I must ask the court's forgiveness and indulgence in this irregular matter. I am bound by word and vow willingly ta be her protector. I cannae serve two masters, and my vow supersedes my promise."

The cacophonous crescendo of outrage was silenced suddenly by the banging of Amergin' staff on the floor. "I hearby dismiss Alexander Malcolm Sinclair, Reliquary, as my proxy. He has served me well in the past and I hereby proclaim his oath fulfilled."

The Caileach held up a hand silencing the dissidents. "Master Myrddin, yer request is approved, though 'afore we continue, ye must name a new body for the office."

"Aye, that I must." He motioned to the crowd and it parted, "I name Tavish Donald Sinclair ta proxy."

Chapter 23

"Welcome all ta the Ban Druidh. We will reconvene at sunset for the conclusion of the ceremony. Priestess and Myrddin, prepare yer proxies."

Brenawyn looked at Amergin expecting guidance, but he thumped his staff on the ground. "Lady of Winter," he bowed low, "I ask that none be allowed ta leave the confines o' the meeting chamber."

"This has never been asked 'afore, Myrddin. What prompts this inquiry? The incantation o' the Ban Druidh opens the doorway and makes safe the passage 'tween our worlds. What makes ye ask that I stay that invitation? T'would be a most grievous insult ta those assembled."

"T'is no' insouciant request I ask. I ken the magnitude and ask it all the same knowing that reparations will be sought against my person."

"Explain yerself."

"All that come are no' true o' heart. Some seek ta subvert."

"Is that no' in the minds o' all who come ta the bargain?"

"If t'were solely ta be the best advantage I'd agree, but this is...something more, something insidious. There is unrest—ye must feel it here, too, in the gloaming."

Caileach paced, clearly considering his word, "For some time I ha' felt an uneasiness, a pervasive weight in the air, like a stillness 'afore a storm. From whence does it originate?"

"I doonae ken, my lady, but stay the invitation til the completion o' the ceremony a' dusk."

"T'would ha' ta be agreed ta."

Brenawyn piped up, "I second the mo…"

Amergin interrupted her with a hand, and Caileach turned to her, bowing.

"For this, priestess, yer second is nay acknowledged. The Myrddin's request must be agreed ta by representatives o' the Tuatha Dé, the Formor, and the Fir Bolg; two affirmations are necessary, three preferable, if only ta assure nay retaliation will ensue."

Cernunnos spoke then. "The Tuatha Dé agree ta terms proposed by Amergin Ambrosius, the Milesian Myrddin."

Caileach tilted her head to acknowledge his second. She turned to the Formor.

"Nay, the Formor doonae agree if the Myrddin cannae gi' accurate account."

"So noted, Ruadan." She pivoted to the Fir Bolg. "One for, one against. What say ye?"

The males conferred, but it was the female who spoke up. "We agree. It matters not, wherst we repose."

"So say ye." She clapped her hands. "Each delegate party will be shown ta a separate antechamber."

Brenawyn turned to rush into Alex's arms, but he caught her and held her at arm's length. "Doonae dae this here. There are too many that will note the vulnerability. Amergin bought us time. We mustnae delay. There's a chance that it can be dealt with quietly still."

The antechamber they were brought to was approximately size of the one with the hot spring, big enough to house two hundred comfortably. She was ushered in first, followed by Amergin and Alex. They took her directly to the far corner of the room, facing the entrance so they had a full view. It was a defensive move, typical gunfighter's stance, back to the wall. Tavish came in next and took to pacing at the door eager for his wife's arrival. When she entered it was in the midst of Liam's guards, whose names Brenawyn still didn't know, but in their time with their custodians, Brenawyn and Isla remained unmolested.

It did not stop Tavish from grabbing the first by the shirt and hitting him square in the jaw. His head rocked back and the others fanned out. Isla ran behind her husband, and Alex jumped into the fray followed by Amergin who ran to meet Isla and bring her back to the relative safety of where Brenawyn stood.

His interlace glowed softly and Brenawyn reached

out to touch his hand. The contact surprised him, and his first reaction was to pull away, but she was insistent and held on. Brenawyn needed to feel his power as a way to access hers. She didn't know the extent of his abilities, but she felt his source and searched for her own. Her interlace flared and his eyes grew wide.

Alex made swift work of the two on the left, but he hung back to let Tavish take his rage out on the two he faced. Even Brenawyn could see that the man was exhausting energy and it was taking entirely too much time to incapacitate the men, but Alex stood as sentinel giving the man leeway.

Still holding Amergin's hand, she saw Alex flex his fingers, she'd seen that move before from him, and she reached out with her senses. He felt his heart race and the building frustration. This needed to be over before Liam and Cormac entered.

Let Tavish deal with it.

Amergin made a noise, and wiggled free of her hold.

Alex pivoted. *Brenawyn get out of my head.*

She persisted, and pushed further. Broken images flashed in her mind: a boy skipping rocks at a lake, her on a stepladder in her grandmother's shop, the flush of instant lust, weightlessness, hunger, salivation, the metallic taste of blood, lust.

Get out of my head! Walls went up and she was

physically pushed back.

Coming too, she shook herself and Amergin helped steady her. "That was no' me. Ye did that all on yer own. It's a slippery slope ye've found. Best no' go where it leads. He'd die a thousand deaths for ye, make no mistake, but allow him his own thoughts. T'is all that he has that he can call his own. Doonae take that from him."

Alex grunted, and jumped in to finish off the last man. Before he could rise completely to his feet to meet Tavish again, Alex grabbed a handful of the man's hair and brought his knee up. There was a satisfying crunch and a burst of blood as the man's nose broke on Alex's knee. He crumpled to the ground, hands clasped over his gushing nose. Tavish rounded on Alex, the fight still in him and took a wild swing. Alex caught his fist and twisted his arm behind his back. "T'is done. Stand down."

But Tavish scrambled to get a hold on Alex's other arm to try to throw him over his shoulder one handed. Alex planted his feet and resisted, exerting more pressure on the arm he still held.

"Man, yer fight is no' with me, and yer wife is safe. Go ta her now." He released the man shoving him away, and Tavish rounded on him."

"Go ta yer wife, man. She needs ye," Alex repeated.

Tavish heaved a breath, and nodded, rubbing at his arm. Isla was bouncing on the balls of her feet in impatience, as soon as she saw that the fight was truly over she ran to him. Tavish caught her when he turned, lifting her off her feet in a one armed embrace. Their reunion was short lived, however, because the great doors were sealed with a boom. Alex whirled around and screamed, "No!"

Brenawyn looked to Amergin to explain.

"Once the doors are sealed they cannae be opened until the appointed time."

"So, Maggie?"

He shook his head, "I doonae ken, lass. I doonae ken."

Alex fell to his knees, his defensive red runes igniting. Brenawyn moved to go to him, but Amergin held her back. "Leave him. He's gathering strength for the coming battle."

Chapter 24

Time stopped. Brenawyn paced the floor, nerves on edge. Isla slept, leaning on Tavish's shoulder on one of the many couches available. Tables were laden with food along the perimeter, replenished she knew not how, but for the amount of food ingested by Amergin, it was a small wonder. She watched him eat an entire ham. He was finishing off a goose currently, sucking the fat off his fingers noisily.

She leaned against the table at which Amergin sat gorging himself.

"He'll maintain that position until it is time. He's gathering energy."

She looked over at Alex, still on his knees. "You've said that. How come you're not doing the same, or showing me how?"

"Och, that last is easy. Ye havenae asked. As ta the other, that's how he chooses to do it. Me? I eat. The sources o' our abilities are different, ye ken. Alexander is a warrior, and his abilities focus on that. He swifter, stronger, and more agile. Because o' it, he can shift faster than e'en I could, and I ha' been alive three o' his lifetimes."

"The ability to shift is bestowed on the Reliquary?"

"Aye, and a few others. I didnae ha' it ta begin with, but ha' retained it after the mantle was passed."

"That doesn't happen all the time?"

Amergin shrugged. "I am the first to ha' survived the transition."

Brenawyn's eyebrows shot up. "Oh!"

"Priestess, ye should eat something."

"I'm not hungry. I can't eat. My stomach is just too upset."

"Ye should eat for the bairn."

She turned, "How did you know? Oh, did Mistress Fordoun tell you?"

Amergin laughed at that. "Ta get that woman ta tell ye anything," he hooted, slapping his leg. "Would take the strength of an entire army a' threat o' torture, even afterward, she'd no' say. Nay, I ken it when ye touched my hand."

"Really?" she looked at her palm.

"Yer heartbeat is strong, but there's an echo o' another underneath fluttering quickly as the hummingbird flies." He pressed on her thumb pad, "I felt it here."

~ ~ ~

Later, a chime sounded and the doors were pulled open. Alex picked up his head and rose to his feet, determined. He went to the threshold and looked out. Brenawyn caught his look of consternation before he wiped his face of all emotion. *Here we go.* He held out a hand to her blocking her from seeing beyond.

"Whate'er happens, ken that I will protect ye with all that I am. That extends ta wee Maggie, too." Brenawyn nodded and tried to get around him, but he stopped her again. "Ask for trial by combat."

She pulled away, but he dug his fingers into her arm trying to get her to comprehend what he wanted her to do. What he needed her to do. "Brenawyn, *a chuisle*, do ye understand what I'm saying? Ye must ask for trial by combat. T'is the only way that I can intervene."

"Trial by … combat? Who will it be with? Liam? Cormac?"

"It doesna matter, Brenawyn. I am afraid t'will be the only way ta save Maggie."

She tore away from him and stumbled to the threshold before he could prevent her seeing. He grabbed at her to pull her in, but she recoiled, screaming in frustration. The chamber had changed. Torches were lit around the center dais illuminating a wood and straw structure. Maggie was there at the base, tied and gagged.

"What the fuck is this?" She stalked out, intent on her destination, but it was Amergin who stopped her this time.

"Get the fuck out of my way, old man."

Alex picked her up, and carried her back. Amergin followed, ordering everyone out of the antechamber.

She rallied against him, pummeling his chest,

jackknifing her legs so he'd lose his grip, but he held on until he dropped her unceremoniously on a divan. "Shut the doors."

She was up in a shot and his defensive scarlet sigils blazed to life. "If ye want ta go ye ha' ta get through me, then Amergin. But yer no' likely ta best us both."

Amergin implored, "Brenawyn, listen ta us. T'is verra important that ye dae."

"What? Do you expect me to just let it happen?"

"Nay, o' course we doonae, but they've orchestrated ta use yer emotions against ye. The Coven is here. They've tried ta get ye o'er ta their side, first with Liam."

She scoffed.

"That bastart, he'll suffer a' my hands 'afore the night is done. I swear ta ye. I will visit vengeance upon his head for the grievous wrongs he committed. But that's a separate issue. Liam is just a man."

Brenawyn nodded but still seethed.

"The Coven tried ta abduct ye in the garden, when yer dog was hurt. They tried to take yer powers in Leo's house, when they gutted me. They tried again in Tannersville. Ye've resisted all. Yer strong. Stronger than ye ken."

She glanced away. "Little good it did."

Alex grabbed her chin to force her to face him, "Hey, hey, look at me! They couldnae dae it, so they went ta where yer vulnerable. They went ta those ye love. Cormac took Maggie."

Brenawyn, "Don't you think I've fucking seen it! I've been helpless, wracked with worry these weeks I've been here. Not knowing were she was. Hating myself for involving her."

Amergin interrupted, "T'is nay yer fault."

"No? Really? Do you honestly believe that?"

"Aye, we both do. We all ha' vulnerabilities." Amergin injected.

"Not you." Brenawyn accused Alex.

He threw a chair across the room and it splintered against the wall. "So sure, are ye about that, hmm?"

"You're what, 600 years old?"

"And in that time, did ye ken I no' formed attachments? Had nay people I cared about? Loved? Did ye think I lived a chastse life? And we're fucking, *aye, yer word that ye love so much*, we're *fucking* back here now. My family still lives. My wife…"

"Yer wife?" Brenawyn blurted.

"Oh? Didnae ken that I was marrit once? Though in truth I should ha' said my ex-wife. She still lives, or at least I think she does, though there's nay way for me ta be sure on that account. I doonae wish her harm, but I doonae want ta see her e'er again."

"Were getting off topic," Amergin cautioned.

Alex nodded, closing his eyes. He gulped and took a measure breath, sighing, "And then there's ye."

"Me? We've known each other for a few short

months."

"Aye, that's the truth, *a chuisle*—blood of my heart. I cannae be the man ye deserve, I ken verra well that ye doonae return my feelings, such as they are, but t'is the truth."

Alex stroked her abdomen with his fingertips. "And the babe." A tear ran down his cheek. "I am laid bare between the two o' ye."

Silence stretched between them but Brenawyn relented and stepped close to him. She reached up to wipe the tear away and sighed, "What do you want me to do?"

~ ~ ~

Caileach reconvened the assembly with a thump of her staff. Circling the center offertory, the Wickerman, she welcomed each race: Fir Bolg, Formor, Tuatha Dé, and the Milesians. The representatives bowed from their waist at mention, and when it was Brenawyn's turn she felt Alex's direction to do the same from his hand's pressure on her shoulder.

The celebrant approached the Fir Bolg first and a representative of the three stepped out and allowed her to lead him around the offertory. She recounted their lineage in Gaelic. Understanding from the repetition of syllables only, Brenawyn figured it was something along the lines of "the father of…the father of," going back to the beginning of time itself. Adhering to the acclaimed oral tradition of the Druids, under any other circumstances, Brenawyn might have had some pity for the lost beauty and the rich history of the storyteller's art; but as it was all she could see was Maggie bound and gagged at the base of the offertory.

The litany went on for an interminable time to the cheers of the Fir Bolg assembled, but eventually the representative was led back to his seat. There was more bowing, and then the woman asked, *"Céard a déarfas tu'?"*

Brenawyn turned her head to Alex in question. He put up a hand telling her to hold her question.

The representative answered, *"Tá sé mar atá tú ag sealaíocht."*

Caileach bowed and then turned to the Formor to begin their lineage account. When she led Ruadan out, Alex bent to whisper into Brenawyn's ear.

"T'is a recounting o' their ancestry. Afterward she asks if she narrated it well. His answer is a formal one o' acknowledgement. Translated it means, 'It is as ye relay.' When it comes time, I will help ye through it. Doonae worry."

Brenawyn gulped. "When do I request…"

His hand tightened on her shoulder, "Ye'll ken when."

From the Formor, the process of naming proceeded to the Tuatha Dé Danann with Caileach leading Finvarra. Before long the woman stood in front of her. Brenawyn stepped out and took the woman's hand. Before she could begin there was movement from the opposite side of the circle, and Ruadan's voice thundered. *"Tá truailliú ann nach mór a cheartú."*

The Caileach patted her hand and led her back to her place before addressing the interruption. "Ambasadóir Ruadan, I ask ye ta speak plain so that the accused can understand yer grievances."

Ruadan moved to the center, foregoing formalities and addressed Brenawyn. "Priestess, ye are a corruption that must be remedied."

Caileach turned to her, "What say you ta these charges, priestess?"

"I am not sure," she said hesitantly.

It was Amergin who clarified, "He means that ye are not worthy o' the title."

Brenawyn spoke out, "With all due respect to your office, Lady of Winter, and to these most sacred proceedings, but who is he to make such accusations? I felt the weight of the mantle of my office the moment I took the blood oath."

"Blood oath?" Ruadan scoffed. "In what circumstances did ye take the oath?"

"My blood was spilled on the banks of the Well of Seagis in Tir-Na-Nog witnessed by Nimue of the Tuatha Dé Danann. Call her to give testimony."

The crowd parted behind Finvarra, Cernunnos,

and Oghma to allow Nimue, the goddess of the moon, to step forward.

Caileach acknowledged her presence, "Is there truth in her words?"

"Labhraíonn sí an fhírinne."

"The assembly accepts the claim and testimony as truth."

Nimue inclined her head and stepped back within the sea of those pressed to get a better view of the proceedings.

The celebrant thumped her staff. "Ambasadóir Ruadan, ye ha' yer proof."

"The Formor doonae accept it."

"So be it." Caileach sighed and turned to Brenawyn.

Before she had a chance to speak, Brenawyn asserted, "I have no need to offer excuses, no patience to explain myself. In the interest of a quick resolution, I ask for trial by combat!"

"Dae ye understand what ye ask?" the celebrant questioned.

Alex nodded to Brenawyn, and she shakily answered in the affirmative.

"Then declare the first contender, priestess."

"First?" She looked back and Alex and Amergin, who both nodded in agreement. "Alexander Sinclair, Druid Reliquary—

Another member of the Formorian emissary spoke up. "As accuser o' the Pretender, the Formor declare

Ruadan the Infiltrator as contender."

Ruadan grunted in satisfaction.

Finvarra interrupted, "Then as safeguard ta ensure the accords o' combat are upheld, I move the assembly ta strip Ruadan o' his immortality."

"The reason?"

"Ne'er in the history o' this assembly ha' a mortal and a god been paired. Level the playing field, else the battle is o'er 'afore it has begun."

"So noted." Caileach thumped her staff on the ground. "Ruadan the Infiltrator, when next ye enter the battlefield ye dae so without the safeguard o' yer immortality."

He looked shocked and turned to his brethren, pleading with them to speak up, but they did not. Crestfallen, he faced the celebrant again and agreed.

"The trial will commence when the field o' battle stands in readiness. Please escort the combatants ta the antechambers."

Brenawyn retired with Alex to their assigned holding area but not before seeing Caileach's interlace ignite and the walls begin to move. A loud grating of stone grinding and moving twenty feet up filled her ears. She saw a ledge forming, but her concerns lay elsewhere. She entered the antechamber and the doors closed behind her.

Brenawyn went to Alex. "Have you ever fought him before?"

"Aye, in a way. I ha' no' thought retribution was coming so soon."

"He is a Formorian. His rudimentary magic is derived from the elements; he'll be good at hand to hand, a virtual juggernaut." Amergin assessed.

Brenawyn made a distressed noise, but Alex squeezed her hand.

"He'll no' be any good with quick movements or tight spaces. He'll no' be able ta call up any additional spells ta distract ye. That's his weakness. Yer no' as physically strong, but yer quicker, more agile, and ha' magic that ye can call ta yer aid."

"Aye."

"Ye need ta make him think he'll win at first. He's an arrogant bastart, that one. He'll make a mistake and let down his guard. That's when ye attack with all ye ha'."

"Why does he hate you so much?"

Alex snickered. "Lass, that is a story for another time. Now we ha' ta think what Cormac's next move is because once the trial begins, things will unfold verra quickly."

"After you win…"

"Wait, lass, e'en as the battle begins Cormac will try ta get ta ye. So ye need ta stay close ta Amergin."

Amergin dug in his bag and extracted Brenawyn's necklace, the Eiliminteach, and the dagger she had last remembered seeing in her grandmother's living room on the night of Alex's last death.

"Where did you get those?"

"Mistress Fordoun. She found them in yer belongings and being the sole o' discretion herself, thought they belied yer position dressed as ye were. She kept them separate and only entrusted them ta me a' the last when we were leaving."

Brenawyn slipped the necklace over her head, nestling the amulet against her skin as Alex told her to do weeks ago. "With everything that was going on I had forgotten that I had them."

"That woman, I swear, has the Sight. A' the last, she came rushing ta me, da ye remember? Forcing them in my hands a feared that ye may be in need o' them." Amergin grimaced, "And here we are. Ye are in need."

Brenawyn looked perplexed. "Where do I…I have no pockets in this thing. No garters. I don't have a place to keep the knife." She held it out to Amergin. "Perhaps you'd better hold onto it for me."

"Och lass. If ye are in need o' it, call it ta ye."

She laughed. "What? I'm not telekinetic."

"Have ye tried?"

"Don't be ridiculous."

Alex and Amergin gave her identical level stares.

"That's possible?"

"Repeat after me. *Teacht dom.*"

"*Teacht dom.*"

"Go o'er there, thinking o' the knife, and recite it."

Brenawyn trekked over to the other side of the room, repeating the phrase.

"Think about the knife. Good. Call it." Amergin instructed.

"*Teacht dom.*" Nothing happened.

"Ye ha' ta think about the knife, first."

"I did."

"Try it again."

She clicked her tongue. "Here knife, come here." She whistled.

The sarcasm was unappreciated by the two men, who both scowled.

"This is nay game." Alex scolded.

She tried again. "*Teacht dom,*" and the knife appeared in her hand. Her eyes grew large with disbelief.

Amergin turned to Alex. "T'is the same spell for calling my clothes after shifting. Use it, man. Nary a man nor woman alive wants ta see yer naked backside. Yer no' a young man any longer."

~ ~ ~

The horn sounded and the doors swung wide. The chamber had changed again, with a balcony stretching the entire circumference of the room. Separate staircases for the four races were packed with onlookers as they ascended. Brenawyn and Amergin were escorted to an area off the main battlefield on the floor. The Wickerman was in the center, with Maggie tied and gagged. Brenawyn had a bad feeling. With the trial about to begin, Caileach thought to leave it where it was, thus further endangering Maggie as the battle raged around her.

Across the field Ruadan was preparing and Cormac, Liam, and another man were with him.

"The lines are drawn." Amergin mused.

"Is that all of them?" Brenawyn asked.

"The Coven has twelve. The Oracle, she's dead. Ruadan, Cormac, Liam, this unnamed man, and seven others."

"So… this won't be over after this?"

"Nay. It has just begun." Alex held her hand, "Listen ta me, Brenawyn. They tried at Lughnasadh and they are trying at Samhain. If they are no' successful a' gaining yer abilities, t'will be another battle at Oimelc, and then an onslaught at Beltane as the window closes on their ambition. The further ye resist the more desperate they will become."

"What happens at Beltane?"

"There are four thresholds that a person new ta the office o' priestess or reliquary must cross. T'is seen as a time o' training, a time when yer abilities grow and mature. With the conclusion o' Beltane, yer abilities will be fully established. They willnae be able ta touch ye after."

"And after, what can I expect?"

"The last priestess…scorched an entire village. Men, women, children…all living things—turned to pillars of ash. She salted the earth and cursed their descendants if any escaped. To this day, no life has e'er returned."

Brenawyn was horrified. "Why?" she asked meekly.

"They made her resort ta using the Rite o' the Phoenix ta give her child ta the universe."

"Alex, wasn't that the story you told me about…"

"Cernunnos' lover? Yes, Brenawyn." he answered pointedly.

She searched out Cernunnos on the balcony above. "That would mean that…*oh, Fuck*!"

A single thump drew her attention to Caileach on the field. There was no time for Brenawyn to think. The trial was starting.

"The Trial of Combat commences. T'will be a battle ta the death. O' the matter in contention, only the truth will be the victor."

Alex kissed Brenawyn full on the mouth but in these last seconds she could feel him shifting just enough to give rise to the predator instincts and heightened senses. She felt the Wolf, Bear, and Leopard stir within his blood. She stepped back, and he drew the long sword from its sheath and stalked out to meet Ruadan.

She had only seen him use his sword one other time, with the constructs his mother, Nimue, created to showcase his abilities. He assumed the first position, the Ochs, sword held level with his ear, tip pointing up tilted toward Ruadan's throat. Ruadan rushed him, and Alex sidestepped. He lowered his weapon to the second position, the Plow, awkwardly. Even though Brenawyn knew it for a ruse, she was scared.

Ruadan rushed him again, Alex sidestepped, but this time he drew first blood, a minor flesh wound, but it enraged the Formorian. Ruadan tossed his sword away, roaring in anger and ran at Alex who shifted sword positions again to the Alber. It looked as if Alex was going to throw his weapon away too, but just as his opponent closed in Alex slashed at his legs, drawing blood again.

Before the next run Alex moved to the Oberhut position. It was the most awkward looking position, exacerbated by the fact that he hadn't moved much. He readied himself to come down from above when Ruadan shifted, bringing him well within the reach of the sword strike. The blade found purchase in the meaty muscle of Ruadan's shoulder, but the close proximity made the effect minimal. Ruadan wrenched the blade out of Alex's hands and tossed it away to clang off the wall nearest Brenawyn and Amergin. Ruadan's hand caught Alex's throat and he pulled him off his feet while his other fist pummeling him with repeated jabs to the ribs. Alex didn't even try to avoid them.

One moment Alex was there, the next he was not, the shift happened so quickly. Brenawyn saw it happen, but it didn't register for what it was. She remembered him telling her that he preferred to shift to animals of the same relative mass because it didn't require an additional expenditure of energy. He never said he couldn't do it. A black rodent dropped from Ruadan's hands, the abrupt shift had apparently taken him by surprise.

Once on the ground, the rodent skittered between his legs and Ruadan pivoted and pursued, trying to stomp on him. Alex's rodent form was too quick, darting into the Wickerman under Maggie's legs. Ruadan having no compunction as to the welfare of the soon-to-be sacrifice stalked to her, but before he could lay a hand on her, a roar of a bear broke the silence.

The bear bounded from around the structure and launched himself at Ruadan. Both crashed to the ground. Ruadan grappled, searching for a good hold, but Alex's claws sliced through skin and organ. He opened his mouth to scream, exposing his neck and the vulnerable carotid artery. Alex sunk his teeth in and held on until the last of Ruadan's convulsions ended. Only when Alex was sure did he release.

Movement from Ruadan's camp was instantaneous. The three men moved in different directions toward a torch. Brenawyn could see their purpose and screamed a warning. Alex shifted back to his human form and tackled Cormac first. They tumbled, fists flying.

It left Liam free to make his move. Brenawyn

vaulted onto the field her interlace flaring to life and Liam mounted the dais to the Wickerman. He turned toward her with a smile playing on his lips as he slowly backed toward the pyre. She slowed, holding her hands out, imploring him to stop.

"Are ye willing ta give up yer powers, Brenawyn?"

"Step away and we'll talk about it."

"It really is too bad that your powers didn't manifest earlier. Things could have been so much different between us."

"Liam, you don't want to do this."

"Why not? Don't you know what's possible, Bren? You have the ability to transcend this mortal coil. You could be revered, worshipped."

"I never wanted that."

"Well, if you don't, then I do. Abdicate your powers, Brenawyn."

"Show me how and you can have them."

Brenawyn didn't see Amergin, but saw the working as it hit Liam square in the chest knocking him flat. The torch tumbled out of his hands and rolled to catch on the straw at the base of the pyre. Brenawyn saw Maggie cower away from it and *whoosh!* The whole pyre, pretreated with pitch, burst into flame. Maggie screamed and Brenawyn rushed to her, oblivious to the flames licking at the ends of her robe. Her interlace flared blindingly and she raised her arms.

The water from the hot spring in the first antechamber burst out of its confines like a loosed dam and flooded the field, dousing the burning Wickerman in a deluge.

Brenawyn scrambled to where Maggie lay unmoving. Her body was contorted and her mouth hung open. Her clothes were burned away and skin charred black. Brenawyn refused to see. She cradled the body, holding it close to her chest.

It was Finvarra, God of the Dead, who approached first to claim her body.

"No! Get the fuck away from us. She'll be fine."

Alex and Amergin came to console her, but all she did was shake her head. "It's my fault. My fault." Brenawyn repeated as she rocked back and forth.

It was the sight of Liam lurking in the shadows that pushed her over the edge. All of her interlace glowed, but seeing him a shift occurred. The blue sigils of healing sapped the luminescence from the others until they were the only ones ignited. She huddled over Maggie's lifeless body and keened, the glow of her sigils matching the decibels of her wail until a soft pop and resulting deep rumble from the ground underneath her, healing light exploded from her chest and washed over Maggie.

Maggie's body seized and bent back, growing rigid as the light was sucked in. Brenawyn could see it still shining from her open mouth, and then she heard the girl gasp. She sunk into Brenawyn's arms, pliant, but her skin still charred and flaking away.

"Amergin, help her."

He came to them and she carefully placed Maggie's body down, intent on leaving her in his capable, healing hands. She had to exact revenge. She couldn't let Liam escape unscathed. She called for her knife, and stalked to where she'd seen him last. The chamber was filling up as the onlookers descended to get a closer look at the scene. Everyone gave her wide berth. She was running now. She passed Tavish, grabbing and unhooking the hatchet at his belt. Now armed with both weapons, she finally saw Liam. Alex had him pinned to the wall, his face already bloody.

"It's only fair, I suppose, that ye've had her. I did take Colleen from you."

"Shut yer mouth, ye willnae speak o' her that way."

"I don't see how you can stop me other than killing me. Tell me, Alexander, who do you prefer? Hmm? Brenawyn, I think. She's a hellcat in bed. Much like those dearg due, wouldn't you agree?"

"Shut yer fucking mouth!" Alex punched him in the jaw.

"Alex?" Brenawyn interjected.

He turned to her.

"What are you doing?"

"Laying vengeance at yer feet."

"Don't. Bring him. He can be of use."

She turned on her heel and Alex followed, Liam in

tow. They neared the dais again, the onlookers parting the way before her.

"Let him go."

"Ye want me ta let him go? But why?"

"Trust me."

By this time, the onlookers—Fir Bolg, Formorians, Tuatha Dé Danann, and the Milesians mixing together—filled the gap. When Alex let Liam go he was confused as to which way to run. He looked one way, his thoughts so loud that Brenawyn could almost hear him reason. Fight through the crowds to go back to the mortal realm or to Tir-Na-Nog?

He made a decision, and bolted. Before Alex reacted, Brenawyn threw the hatchet at Liam's retreating form. It flew end over end and found its home deep between Liam's shoulder blades. He fell to his knees, reaching behind him in an attempt to grasp the handle. Blood spurted from his back as Brenawyn rounded his dying form. Smiling down on him, she touched his cheek, and brushed his hair off his forehead. She leaned down to kiss his lips, and he relaxed, giving himself over to the tenderness. He opened his mouth wider and she stroked his tongue with her own, tempting him to be bold in his last moments. He extended his tongue and she seized it, sucking provocatively. Then her fingers cradling his cheeks became a vice, her lips hard and punishing as she sucked whatever remained of his life force from him. He felt himself dry and wither under her, his last thought on his cockstand.

She let his lifeless body fall to the ground and wiped her mouth, intent on Maggie. The girl was alive, but barely, each breath torture for her burnt lungs. The life force of Liam would go to good use in repairing some of the damage but she needed more. She scanned the area. No one would be willing. If she could only locate Cormac or that other man. Their lives were forfeit having revealed their intent. They wouldn't be welcomed in Tir-Na-Nog, and would be on the run in the mortal realm. That was the better chance for them anyway, with their ability to hide in time, but first things, first.

Amergin scooted over to give Brenawyn access. She bent down grimacing. To do this she had to cause Maggie more pain. There was no other way. "I'm so sorry." She pinched Maggie's nose and opened her mouth. She put her lips to Maggie's and blew forcefully just once until her chest felt tight and she was out of breath. She lifted her head and placed her other hand on Maggie's mouth to not allow Liam's life force to escape.

She held this position until Maggie started to squirm under her hands. "Amergin, hold her."

Amergin did as instructed, and the charred bits of Maggie's skin flaked away; the sores scabbed and flaked off too, leaving shiny scar tissue. Only then did Brenawyn remove her hands. Maggie gasped, and gulped in air.

A voice behind her asked, "Do you need more?"

Brenawyn turned to see the other man who had been with Liam and Cormac earlier. He was young; he would do. "Yes."

He nodded, approaching, "My life for hers." He fell to his knees.

Maggie's hand flailed toward him, and he caught it. He caressed the back of her hand, kissing her knuckles.

"I am so sorry. I never wanted you to get hurt."

"Andy," she whispered as a tear escaped to run down her cheek.

He caught it with a knuckle, and turned to Brenawyn. "Take my life for hers."

It was all Brenawyn needed to hear, and she closed in on his mouth taking his life force the same way she had taken Liam's, but this was freely given. The strength of it staggered her, almost pushing her back, but he was the one to reach out and clasp her so she could take all he had to give. When she laid the dried husk that once housed this man, she understood sacrifice. She turned and breathed his life into Maggie.

Mottled scar tissue smoothed and pinked. Hair grew, first in peach fuzz on her arms and legs, then eyelashes, eyebrows; and then on her head, a rich brunette.

Caileach appeared and covered Maggie with her own cloak. Brenawyn smiled up at her in thanks.

Before she moved back into the crowd, Brenawyn stopped her with a hand.

"I know that I will have to answer for my actions, but I ask that it wait until she's healed enough."

"Doonae worry, priestess. All is well. The order o' events may ha' differed, but all honors were observed."

Chapter 25

Cernunnos entered the antechamber with a scroll, but was stopped just beyond the threshold by Alex.

"She is saying goodbye to Maggie."

The god nodded his head.

"The declaration terms?"

Cernunnos held up the roll, "All she need dae is sign."

"When is the first meeting set for?"

"In the next phase o' the moon ta establish rapport…"

"And for assessing leverage." Alex finished the god's statement matter-of-factly. "Political intrigue," he scowled, "not my strong suit.

"Aye, I ken verra well, but t'is the way true advancement happens."

"Verra diplomatic o' ye, Cernunnos. What dae ye hope ta gain?"

"E'erything, but t'is nay compromise that way." The god smirked, "ye'll ha' ta wait."

Aerten's warning sprang to mind in that instant. *Danger surrounds. Trust neither god nor mortal.* Alex kept his own counsel.

"And Cormac?" Alex inquired intentionally changing the subject.

"He slipped notice, but now there's no place he can hide."

"Dae the prophecies still sing that he'll be the next Reliquary?"

"Aye, that they dae, and t'is a wonder how t'will come ta be."

"Then he'll no' be gone for verra long."

Cernunnos cleared his voice, stopping Alex from interrupting with a hand to his forearm. "Priestess, I ha' someone who wishes ta see ye."

Brenawyn looked up and sighed, "Can't it wait?"

"No. Ye'll want ta see her." He motioned for the woman to enter.

She was cloaked, her face in shadow from the deep cowl.

"Yes? How may I help you?"

The woman threw the hood back and both Brenawyn and Maggie gasped as they rose to their feet.

"Nana! What happened to your eye?"

The End

Read on for a sneak peek at the fourth book in the Celtic Prophecy series: *Amergin's Covenant*

AMERGIN'S COVENANT

Chapter 1

Leo parked her car in the police station's lot and prayed to whatever god was listening for some good news. She got out; the hinges of the car's door resisted until huffing with effort she applied more pressure and the door slammed shut, rattling the window in its frame. She opened the door again as wide as it would go, and slammed it. The hinges squeaked in opposition again, but the exertion somehow lightened her load. She repeated it three more times until she caught the side glance of another person walking, swifter now, to enter the building.

She decided that she didn't care. People entered a police station for three reasons: if they worked there, but this man didn't have on the telltale uniform that all officers wore. The second was to bail someone out of jail or make a court appearance, and if that was the case, the man had no right to judge her little tantrum. And the third, well the third was what brought her...to get an update on an investigation. If she'd thought about it more there were other reasons, someone filing a complaint or a soon to be teacher getting fingerprinted. She thought Brenawyn had had to do that before getting her job. It made sense working with children and all, but she was not in a generous mood today to wax poetically about the foot traffic a police station sees.

She strained to open the heavy door against the wind, but the handle slipped out of her hands before she had it open halfway. She was quick enough to shove the end of her cane, blocking the door from closing completely and gripping the edge of the door. She yanked it open, briefly noting the dent at the bottom of the metal cane as she entered the building.

Passing a row of plastic chairs lined up on either side of the door, she approached the desk. The policewoman behind the glass looked up. "May I help you?"

"Yes. Good morning. I'm here to see Officer Simmons."

The woman picked up her phone, covering the mouthpiece. "Please have a seat; the officer will be right out."

Leo trudged to an open chair on the opposite side of the door from the man who witnessed her episode in the parking lot. She sat with a huff, putting her purse on her lap, facing the door that led back into the precinct. To her right was a hallway that led down to other offices and the small courtroom.

The door in front of her opened setting off a buzzer alarm. It was Simmons, who came to help her up. "Ma'am, I would have come to the house. You needn't have come all the way."

"I know it is more convenient for you to do so."

"It generally is more of a comfort to the family members."

"So you don't run the risk of having hysterical old women." She sighed, and he stopped. Closing her eyes to squeeze out the tears that had welled in the corners, she felt the fat drops roll down her cheeks. He wiped one away with his knuckle and grabbed a box of tissues as he steered her to an empty office. He leaned out to give an instruction, as she settled in one of the chairs tossing her purse on the table. Her cell phone spilled out and the custom case that Brenawyn had specially made from a photo her and Spencer reminded Leo of her glaring omission.

On that fateful day after she lost everything, Leo didn't know what to do, how much to reveal, or what to report. She decided to fill out a missing person's report for Maggie O'Neil, an employee and friend of the family—her granddaughter's friend, after rehearsing in her mind what she would relay. She made up a fictitious story about why they were at the

Caverns—research for a blog post on her company's website, particulars of which would check out at all points. She made sure the explanation of the area and the physical description of the man who took her were acutely detailed. Maggie was abducted, but Brenawyn was not.

Brenawyn went willingly to a place where no amount of detective work would ever find her. Leo opted not to report her as missing and it was killing her. She'd failed her granddaughter again, just like she had always done.

"Ma'am," Simmons started, but was interrupted by a knock on the door, another officer holding a cup of coffee. He was granted entrance and the man put it down in front of Leo, "Milk, no sugar."

"Thank you," she said as she touched his hand.

He squeezed her fingers and gave her a small smile before he left closing the door behind him.

"There haven't been any new developments."

"The woods, they were searched again?"

"Yes, ma'am. The woods, the motel, the Caverns. There was…nothing found that connects to Maggie's abduction."

"Did you search the entire system? It's extensive."

"That's ongoing. The local police have finished their investigation and ruled it out, a manpower issue really."

Leo slumped in her chair.

"Wait," he petitioned, "outside spelunkers were brought in, on a separate issue, but they've been apprised and will report anything they find to the police there. Once they have, they'll contact us."

"That's it then?" Leo didn't need to hear his answer, it was written all over his face.

"I'm sorry I don't have better news."

"It's been forty-six days. What am I supposed to do?"

~ ~ ~

Spencer nosed his way out the front door as Leo opened it, pushing his barrel chest through to prance around the front porch searching. She didn't try to stop him anymore. He wasn't going to run, so she held the door, and watched him race down the steps to *her* car parked in the driveway. The dog circled, his usual path, jumping up at last to put his great paws on the driver side window of the empty car. It was too much to bear, her loss too deep, to hear that they were scaling back the search for fiscal reasons. Leo couldn't hold it together any longer, so when Spencer returned Leo's wracking sobs were added to the dog's pitiful cry.

As she was leaving Simmons had offered a different kind of comfort, pushing business cards of counseling services and support groups on her. Now that she thought on it, Leo caught side glances that they gave each other while she was there, it was all becoming so patronizing. She didn't want to move on, if that were even possible. She didn't want to share her hurt. To admit to being selfish and deciding not to tell Brenawyn everything a decision that led to this end. It was her fault. Even if she managed to sidestep the details she couldn't hear of another parent's loss. She had nothing to give them, no words of comfort; no shoulder to cry on, so focused was she on her own pain and guilt.

During the day managing the loss was easier. She was productive. What was she to do now? She'd made a habit of searching for answers, mostly focusing on Maggie's disappearance. She harangued and harassed the detectives on a daily basis by phone, opting to only physically go down to the station once or twice a week. They could still track her if they found a lead. That bastard took her to use against Brenawyn when the time was right. So looking for Maggie was looking for Brenawyn.

Leo labored down the hallway, each step she took harder until she came to the doorway of Brenawyn's room. The threshold was an invisible barrier she had to force her way through. Once inside, the emptiness, the loneliness, and the guilt crashed in on her. It hobbled her.

She turned back the covers, and laid her head on the pillow. She couldn't smell Brenawyn's shampoo any longer or the floral body spray she used. It had worn off, but she still didn't take the sheets off to wash. Then her scent would be gone for good.

She woke sometime later, to swollen eyes, headache… and the feeling of someone watching her. It was a familiar enough feeling lately, one she'd gotten used to even. Spencer sprawled out along her back, a warm comfort in her sadness, snoring gently. If there was truly someone there, the dog would sense it.

Look for Book Four of The Celtic Prophecy Coming in 2018

A Note from the Author

These past years have been exciting as I continue to explore the world of publishing and marketing my fantasy series, *The Celtic Prophecy*. Since the release of the first book, *Fate's Hand,* I've learned the most rewarding aspect of this venture has been building a relationship with my readers. In my quarterly newsletters I will be sending out alerts to sales, contests, and new releases. By going to my website, https://melissamacfie.com and subscribing to my newsletter you will receive an advance short of the next novel in The Celtic Prophecy series, *Amergin's Covenant.* The short preview should be ready for release in early spring 2018. You can also connect with me on Facebook and Twitter at: http://bit.ly/2B0o5Bq and http://bit.ly/2k7jvXo where I periodically publish excerpts, list my appearances, and giveaways.

A review is the most valuable gift you can give an author. Honest reviews are an invaluable tool for authors, helping them to become recognized for their work and helping them to connect with readers who are looking for new authors and interesting new books to read. If you enjoyed this book, I would whole-heartedly appreciate it if you'd take the time to leave a review when you reach the review link at the end of this book. If you do write one, please send me an email at melissa.macfie@yahoo.com so I can thank you personally.

Acknowledgements

Artistic license was used in choosing the gods featured in this novel. While all of Celtic origin, they are not from the same country. This was intentional to diversify names. A list of gods and their specific origins are in the glossary.

I would like to acknowledge the aid I received from the Irish Translation Forum on the Irish Gaelic Translator website. Their translations lend a nuanced authenticity to this novel. The responsibility for any incorrect usage or phrasing falls to me. Also, the unflagging support I've received from the writing community, specifically Madeline Martin, Krista Venero, Melissa Lummis, Angel Martinez, and Lisette Kristensen. Whether they realize it or not, by taking time out of their busy schedules to answer a question, feature my books in their newsletter, schedule author take-overs and appearances, or organize giveaways, they have had a positive impact on my life as a writer.

Writing is mainly a solitary experience because stories in their entirety reside in our minds; but it is through support groups such as Books Go Social and Indie Author Support administered by Lawrence O'Brien and Krista Venero respectively, I know that I am not alone.

Lastly, I would like to acknowledge my editor and publisher, Karen Hodges Miller of Can't Put It Down Books, without whose guidance and friendship I would not be where I am today.

Glossary

Celtic Gods, Goddesses, Creatures, and Places

Addanc: Welsh primordial giant

Aine: *(AHN yuh)* Irish goddess for fertility

Aerten: *(EYER ten)* Cornish, Welsh goddess of fate

Agrona: Celtic goddess of strife and slaughter

Amergin: (AYV-r-ghin) Milesian bard and Druid who sang a magical song that allowed his people to land safely in Ireland

Badb: *(Bahv)* Irish goddess of war, often assumes the form of the raven

Belanus: Celtic god of light

Blodevweld: *(blo-DOY-weth)* Betrayed her husband by supernatural means which led to his death.

Bres: *(BRESH)* Tyrannical ruler of the Tuatha Dé, defeated at the second battle of Magh Tuireadh

Caer Ibormeith: *(Keer YEW mayth)* Pan-Celtic goddess of dreams and prophecy

Caileach: *(COY Ick) Scottish and Irish goddess of Winter, depicted as having a blue face*

Conmaicne Rein: The mountain of debarkation for the Tuatha Dé Danann.

Cernunnos: *(KER noo nohs)* Pan-Celtic god of the hunt

Danu: Mother of the Tuatha Dé Danann; Mother Earth

Dearg due: (*DAH-ruhg DU-ah*) Irish female faerie known for seducing human men

Dian Cecht: *(DIE-an KET)* god of healing and

regeneration

Finvarra: *(VEEN varra)* Irish High King of the gods

Fir Bolg: *(FEAR-bolg)* Settlers to Ireland who lived peacefully until the coming of the Tuatha Dé Danann and the first battle of Magh Tuireadh.

Formor: Magical race who settled in Northern Ireland. Fought against the Tuatha Dé Danann in the second battle of Magh Tuireadh.

Gancanagh:*(Gan-Kana)* Irish male faerie known for seducing human women, said to emit an addictive toxin

Magh Tuireadh: *(Moy Tirra)*Three battles fought over lifetimes, the first between the Fir-Bolg and the Formorians, the second between the Formorians and the Tuatha Dé Danann, and the third between the Tuatha Dé and the Milesians; all for the land of Ireland.

Mandred: Cornish god, draws the All Power to the one who speaks his name

Milesians: The last group of settlers to come to Ireland. After the third battle of Magh Tuireadh, a truce is made where they would occupy the upper world, whereas the Tuatha Dé, the world below.

Neit: *(NYIT)* Irish god of battle

Nimue: *(NIM oo ay)* Cornish, Welsh goddess of the moon

Nuada: *(NEW-ah)*Twice king of the Tuatha De' Danann

Oghma: *(OH-wam)*, Scottish/Irish god of

communication and writing; known for inventing writing. In the Celtic Prophecy series, the god of memory.

Ratis: Anglo-Celtic goddess of protective fortifications

Ruadan: a Formorian, sent by his father, Bres, to spy on the Tuatha Dé Danann.

Sidhe: *(She)* Irish descendents of the Tuatha Dé Danann

Sluagh: *(Slau)* restless spirits of the dead; in Fate's Hand, embodied as hounds

Taliesin: *(tal-YES-in)* Welsh god of magic, music, poetry, wisdom, and writing

Taranis: *(TA ran is)* Continental goddess of death to whom sacrifices were offered.

Tir-Na-Nog: *(TIER na noog)* realm of the gods

Tuatha Dé Danann: *(TOO-ha dey DAHN-en)* Children of the goddess Danu

Gaelic Words and Phrases

a chuisle: (*a khish la*) term of endearment meaning my heart.

Eiliminteach: *(EE le men tie k) Elemental*

labhraíonn sí an fhírinne: she speaks the truth

teacht dom: Come to me

Fire Feasts

Samhain: (*SAH wen*) Celebrated on October 31 marking the beginning of winter

Oimelc: (*I melg*) Celebrated on February 1 marking the beginning of spring

Beltaine: (*BEY al TIN ah*) Celebrated on May 1 marking the beginning of summer

Lughnasadh: (*LOO nah sah*) Celebrated on August 1 marking the beginning of autumn

References

Black, Susa Morgan. "Deeper into Samhain." *The Order of Bards, Ovates, and Druids* . http://www.druidry.com/druid-way/teaching-and-practice/druid-festivals/ Samhain/deeper-samhain. 28 November 2017.

"Cambridge Songs," Music and Poetry: Fraternal Twins." *Poetry Through the Ages.* http://www.webexhibits.org/poetry/explore-21_song_examples.html. 28 November 2017.

Celtic Gods and Goddesses. http://www.joellessacredgrove.com/Celtic/deities.html 22 June 2016.

Celtic Shamanism. http://www.druidry.org/library/members-articles/ shamanism-celtic-world. 5 July 2016.

Henley, W. E. "Invictus." 1888. https://www.poemhunter.com/ poem/invictus/ 26 November 2017.

Percival, Barbara. "From Paganism to Christianity." https://www.academia.edu/448782/From_Paganism_to_ Christianity. 31 October 2017.

"Races." *Magic and Mythology*. http://www.shee-eire.com/Magic&Mythology/Races/ Page1.htm. 13 June 2016.

Robinson, Melia. "15 Irish Sayings Everyone in America Should Use." 14 March 2015. http://www.businessinsider.com/funny-irish-sayings-2015-3. 2 December 2017.

Spence, Lewis. *Druids: Their Origins and History*. United States of America. Barnes & Noble Books. 1995.

Squire, Charles. *Celtic Myths and Legends*. Bristol. Parragon. 1998.

Wood, Juliette. *The Celtic Book of the Living and Dying: The Illustrated Guide to Celtic Wisdom*. New York. Chartwell Books, Inc. 2012.

About the Author

For most of her life, Melissa Macfie has pursued artistic endeavors such as drawing, painting, and sculpting. She holds a M.Ed. in English Education from the Graduate School of Education at Rutgers University, and has spent the last eighteen years as a public school English teacher. She lives in New Jersey with her husband, Donald. Their children, Elizabeth and Donald, are grown and pursuing their own dreams.

www.ingramcontent.com/pod-product-compliance
Lightning Source LLC
Chambersburg PA
CBHW021956170626
46808CB00001B/173